Board to
Death

Board to
Death

CJ Connor

Kensington Publishing Corp.
kensingtonbooks.com

KENSINGTON BOOKS are published by

Kensington Publishing Corp.
119 West 40th Street
New York, NY 10018

ISBN: 978-1-4967-4223-0 (ebook)

ISBN: 978-1-4967-4222-3

First Kensington Trade Paperback Printing: September 2023

10 9 8 7 6 5 4 3 2 1

Printed in the United States of America

To Mom and Dad

If you're reading this, Dad, you can't just ask me,
"Who is the murderer at the end?" I dedicated the
book to you.
Now you have to read it.

Chapter 1

When I was younger, the best part of working at my dad's board game shop Of Dice and Decks was how easily I could get away with reading books through my shift. I'd hole myself up in the staff room with a stack of Isaac Asimov books half as tall as I was and, when Dad came to slap my wrists (metaphorically, of course), I'd say, "Maybe you should pay me minimum wage if you want to motivate me."

Now, of course, the in-store café was a much bigger perk. And one that I'd taken advantage of nearly every day since returning home to Salt Lake City a couple months ago with little to my name but the stack of books I'd accumulated during my time as a professor, my dignity (questionable), and a raging caffeine addiction.

It was the little things, as they say.

I sipped my Earl Grey latte—iced and with a little whipped cream on the top, because I was trying to get into the self-care movement in a way that didn't involve spending too much of my credit card limit on sweaters for my dog. I manned the cash register as if I were a captain surveying his sinking ship. Too often, when I managed the store finances (or at least attempted to with that same brain of mine that got a D-minus in pre-calc), that's what it felt like.

At two months back in my hometown Salt Lake City, I

worried most days that I would run the board game shop Dad spent over thirty years building into the ground. Hence the standing uncomfortably behind the cash register. Hence the latte. Not that the caffeine did me much favors; with what it offered in terms of comfort, it took away with twitchiness.

Of Dice and Decks looked the same as it did when I'd left it last to "find my destiny" or at least a stable career after finishing my PhD and saying goodbye to working at the shop through my whole childhood and every summer after leaving home. Every corner of the shop was stuffed with rows of board and card games. You could find party and family games as well as more niche items like minifigures used for the more complex games and Dungeons & Dragons rule books. If you could play it, it took up nearly overflowing space here. Our organization style was, in a word, *precarious*. If it could be said that we had an organization style at all. It had never been Dad's strong suit, though the customers never faulted him for it.

It was a place where you could spend hours perusing the shelves and always find something new, something that sparked your attention in a way it hadn't before.

At some point nearly a century ago, the building had (like so many stores in the Sugar House neighborhood of Salt Lake) started life as a one-floor, three-bedroom cottage. When Dad began leasing the place in the eighties, however, it had already been renovated to function as a small store with a kitchen.

There were two main rooms: one spacious-as-one-could-get-in-small-spaces front room for browsing and another with five circular tables (the best shape for playing most anything) that customers could use to play the games we had available to try out or rent by the hour for gaming groups and freelancing space.

Only two or three customers lingered around that area

midday, as it was now. More flocked around those tables in the evenings, when roleplaying groups came to host their campaigns or we held themed nights (or themed weekends, in the case of the infamous and only-once-attempted Risk tournament).

A staff-only door behind the gaming tables led to a storage room that made the rest of the shop look as minimalistic as an IKEA catalog, thanks to Dad's near-legendary lack of organization skills.

With an espresso machine and a minor renovation to create a pass-through window from the kitchen to the front room, Of Dice and Decks ran a café for patrons, which sold mainly "healing potions" (herbal teas) and "power-ups" (caffeinated drinks). The smell of coffee gave the shop a lulling sort of feel (for me, at least, though some of our Mormon patrons tended to look at it like a vampire in a blood bank who had sworn off drinking the stuff).

Besides the few customers using the gaming room, we'd hit an afternoon lull. At the moment, there were no customers in the front room. The barista, Sophie Vaughn, leaned against her window, eyebrows raised over her glasses. "Now's your chance to step out behind the register and make yourself approachable."

Sophie, whose hair had been buzzed as long as I'd known her (and she'd run the café since the nineties, long enough that I could remember her picking me up from preschool when Dad was busy manning the shop), usually donned a T-shirt of the geeky variety. The idea, according to her, was that would get the customers to smile and, ultimately, buy a drink. It tended to work in her favor.

Today, it was a tank top with the bunny from *Monty Python and the Holy Grail* ready to attack. An effective choice. Nerds loved quoting Monty Python, and from there, it only took a few changes of conversation topics to convince them that they needed a coffee.

It stared back at me menacingly, as if it would indeed attack were I not a sufficient enough store manager. I'd say Dad was right and that I should have gone to business school, except that he'd encouraged me the moment I finished college to forget grad school and run the game shop with him.

"In your opinion," I said, "how necessary would that be?"

"Not mandatory. *Nothing's* mandatory. But conversation's better for selling games." Sophie frowned. "You're not scared of the customers, Ben . . . are you?"

It took me a while to answer. Shoving my hands in my pockets was much easier.

"What if," I muttered, just loud enough that she'd have a chance at hearing me, "they don't like me so much that I ruin the whole business?"

"For heaven's sake, Ben, you're thirty. You're too old to be shy."

Thirty, yes—as of today, in fact. But I had no interest in correcting her. It would only make me seem self-conscious about my age, and I was trying very hard not to be. My goal was to not have thirty be a milestone birthday but to have it pass quietly, and without the mysterious back pain every Instagram meme seemed to promise would follow once I hit it.

"It's not shyness. It's self-preservation. Look at me. You think someone like me had a pleasant time in high school?"

She gave me a look, sizing up my messy haircut courtesy of Bargain Clips (trademark "It's Adequate!") and my jacket with the useless patches at the elbow. It had been sensible enough when I was an adjunct professor. Now, it just made me self-conscious that I was nearing the age where people start to have "midlife crises" instead of the friendlier, almost fun-sounding "quarter-life crises."

"I don't know how to answer that," she said, "but I imagine you spent a considerable amount of it playing games."

"Gaming is one thing. Making a good impression is another. What if I make a fool of myself and we lose customers?"

"I feel like we've been having this conversation every day for the past month." Sophie made a shooing motion with her hand. "Your dad may be prickly, but at least he chats up the customers. You need to do the same if you want to make money. You do want that, don't you?"

"All right, all right." I made a show of stepping away from the register. "I'll hang around the shop front, try to make myself useful. Is that what you want?"

"It is," she said. "Now uncross your arms. Customers won't approach you unless your body language invites them to."

I grumbled, even though I knew she was right. I had a shop to run, and unless we couldn't afford rent in the future (a future that seemed worryingly nearer every day), that would not change. Thanks to all the tech start-ups turning the nearby Utah County into what people who had majored in much more practical things than me called the "Silicon Slopes," affording rent in Salt Lake City was an increasingly tough feat.

I also had to give her credit—her advice worked. Standing among the board games instead of the cash register (and, yes, uncrossing my arms), I saw that customers actually approached me. They asked me questions about the games and, despite my rising nervousness talking to people I didn't know, I found that board games were the one topic besides books I could hold a conversation on.

Over the next few hours, I sold a copy of Apples to Apples to a rambunctious family of six and troubleshot an overly complex adventure game that came in a box thicker than Dwayne "The Rock" Johnson's chest.

"I'll admit," I said as I picked up a miniature figurine of an alien, "I know this one's popular right now, but I haven't played it. Did you bring in its instruction manual?"

The customer gave me a weak smile that seemed more

pained than one should be while discussing board games. He then handed me a booklet that was so extensive, it would make George R.R. Martin tempted to pass it off as the next *Game of Thrones.*

I gulped and worked harder at deciphering the text than I had at defending my doctoral thesis. After some heated brainstorming and several YouTube tutorials, we could theorize how in the world it was meant to be played. He even bought a few extra figurines for my trouble.

A little before lunchtime, a woman and a girl half her height came in. Them I knew. Her name was Dr. Britt Petras. Her wife, Yael Flores, ran a cinnamon roll delivery shop called Nice Buns several blocks down the street. Utahns loved few things more than they loved home-delivered baked goods, and Yael's shop never had to worry about rent.

Dr. Petras was a medieval history professor at the University of Utah—and she had the prematurely gray hair paired with outrageous sweaters to prove the stress and eccentricity a career in academia had thrust upon her. Today, she wore a loud purple one with a snail illustration in the middle of it. The girl with her dressed similarly.

While she was finishing her dissertation at the nearby Westminster College, Dad would pay Dr. Petras to tutor me, from third grade reading assignments all the way to AP English. I credited her with my passing the test as well as my decision to later become an English professor—even if I had only been one for five years post-graduation. I'd never really known my mom, nor much about her besides that she and Dad were happier apart, but I'd always had Dr. Petras to turn to for academic (and very occasionally personal) advice.

Over the past few weeks, she'd come into the shop regularly—sometimes to test out a new game, and sometimes just to catch up. I appreciated the familiar face. Little about Of Dice and Decks itself had changed over the years, and neither had I. I'd never been one with a knack for chatting with people I didn't know.

I checked the clock. "Thursdays at eleven, on the dot. Are you sure you're not a witch?"

"Depends on who's asking," said Dr. Petras. "But Bea's been convinced she's a demigod lately, so you're not far off."

Bea clutched what appeared to be a weathered book in the Percy Jackson series. The cover only just hung in there, thanks to the duct tape keeping it in place. "Water damaged" would have been a gentle way of putting it.

In short, it was loved in the way that all books only could hope to be.

I smiled. Percy Jackson was published past my childhood, but I had once been small enough that my entire world revolved around a fictional one. I'd dreamed as a child of becoming a wizard pondering in some magical library over arcane lore, and my brief time as a professor hadn't seemed so far off. If you ignored all the griping about the limited insurance options available to adjunct professors, which I doubted wizards had to do.

Reading was still one of my favorite forms of escapism, up there with running (for sport) and running (away from my problems).

Ultimately, I'd done my dissertation on the influences and beginnings of the modern fantasy genre. In the few years since graduating, I'd taught a number of generals but also courses that allowed me to indulge in my inner nerd, like *Introduction to Tolkien Studies* and *Philosophy and Metaphysics of the Portal Fantasy*.

As far as secondary careers went, "board game shop owner" fit me well enough.

"Bea's your niece, right?" I asked.

Dr. Petras snorted. "Really, you're too flattering. She's my granddaughter."

"We're looking for a copy of Rummikub," Bea added.

"Rummikub." I rubbed my chin in thought, then pointed in the direction of the family game section. "We should have a copy in stock. If not, I can order one for you."

"Ah, thank goodness," said Dr. Petras. "I worried that you'd only have the obscure games in stock, but I wanted to check here before stooping low enough to visit Walmart."

We'd lost enough of our customers to Walmart, or worse, Amazon, as it was. Not that I could blame them, of course, but it stung nonetheless when mentioned to my face.

"No need to do that," I said mildly as they followed me to the shelf. "We've got plenty of the classics."

It took me a few moments of scrambling, but I found the game they were looking for. It was behind five copies of Candyland, each of them dustier than the last. Kids were getting too sophisticated for Candyland. These days, it seemed like they went straight for Clue.

"Wonderful!" Dr. Petras held the game out and beamed. "I used to play this with my great-grandma, let's see . . . forty years ago? How has it been so long? It's silly, but I've been waiting for one of my grandkids to be old enough so I could teach it to them."

"Do you think she's ready?"

"I am," said Bea. "And I can hear you."

"She's smart," agreed Dr. Petras. "Her mom said she finished the library's summer reading program this year in, oh, three weeks."

I pretended to gasp. "Three weeks! You're a genius. How'd you manage that so fast?"

"You get a book if you win," added Bea. "Of course I hurried. Hello, Grandma Britt! Free books!"

Grandma Britt. It was hard for me to hide my smile as I checked them out at the cashier's station, along with a few treats they had picked out by the front. Those were easily our most popular items, as no board game night is complete without a snack. I felt the warm fuzzies that made me feel better about leaving my (if not comfortable, then predictable) teaching job.

Board games brought people together. They were the best thing I knew for loneliness or a longing for connection. I'd never been the best at small talk or making new friends, but board games seemed to get rid of all the awkwardness in favor of bonding over a shared passion. It was nice to facilitate that instead of arguing with a freshman on whether I could be a legitimate English professor and hate Hemingway.

The answer was yes, and only too easily.

"Oh, to be young and spend an evening on a family game night after finishing the summer reading program," remarked Sophie after they'd left.

"I'd settle for a day at the school book fair and unlimited spending money." I ran my fingers through my hair. "Man, what I'd give to be in 2002 for a night, trying to work out Settlers of Catan with my dad."

"Is he coming in the shop this week?"

I froze. "Depends on whether he's up for it, but yes. He's scheduled tomorrow, I think."

"Oh. Right. He doing okay?"

"Why don't you ask him when he comes in?"

My dad was, after decades of putting full (and often overtime) work weeks into the board game shop of his dreams, working part-time.

"I try to, but Martin—I mean, your dad—always avoids my questions," she said. "And I don't want to make him talk about it if he doesn't want to. But I still care about him, you know?"

I looked away. It was hard for me to talk about Dad. I was still figuring out how to do it without getting caught in my emotions.

"He's, you know . . . hanging in there. We're lucky the doctors caught it early. But then not so lucky, since we only knew what signs to watch for because it runs in the family."

"I get that. It's like that with my mom sometimes. I'm glad she still remembers me and my sisters, but the Alzheimer's takes so much of her away from me. It's not fair getting older, is it?"

I cleared my throat, as it was feeling too tight for my liking. It was still hard for me to talk about Dad's condition, even if it was somewhat expected.

"Maybe not. But he always says it beats the alternative. And it gave me an excuse to come home, at least."

Never mind that I still felt so guilty about leaving at all in the first place. Still, what could I have done? Hard enough being openly gay in Utah now. Unthinkable even ten, fifteen years ago. You can only take so many people telling you that you wouldn't go to heaven before you started believing it. Especially when you're young.

"He's around the usual retirement age, isn't he? Maybe that would be good for him."

He was. Not that it meant much. Convincing Dad to retire was an easier thing to say than do because in practice, it would be impossible.

"That would require convincing him to do that in the first place," I said, rubbing the bridge of my nose. "Don't think I haven't tried. Sometimes I wonder who's his actual favorite child: me or the shop."

Before she could say anything else, a voice that cut through the air like a rusty knife right between the shoulder blades interrupted our conversation. "Hey! Mr. Rosencrantz Junior, right? You look just like your dad. You got his ears, didn't you?"

Chapter 2

❧

I spun around and tried to keep my expression calm, despite the somersaulting in my chest that I'd only ever felt in two situations: unpleasant social interactions and that one time when I was ten and went on the Tower of Terror in one of the few family vacations Dad could afford to take.

Nobody, not even my former students, called me "Mr. Rosencrantz." That, as they say, was my father. If anything, I was technically "Dr. Rosencrantz"—though I usually just had my students call me Ben. The full "Doctor" always made me worry I'd find myself in an emergency situation where someone needed an MD and I'd have to bear the bad news that I'd studied C. S. Lewis, not cardiology.

Whoever this person was, they clearly knew of me, but they did not know me. And those were always the most fraught conversations I had.

"It's just Ben," I said stiffly.

"C'mon, Ben! Sit with me. I'll buy you a coffee. Unless you're a Mormon. Then I'll buy you a coffee but promise not to tell your bishop."

The person who had called to me was sitting in the gaming room, and I could just see him waving to me through the open door. His legs were propped up on one of the tables. He seemed at least a decade older than the two others next to him, and they were all sitting with strange expressions on their faces.

What was that—awe? Did I even want to know what one would have to do to make collegiate board game enthusiasts awestruck? I answered that for myself quickly: no, I certainly did not. It couldn't bode well, whatever it was, and I preferred to avoid things that would make my life uncomfortable. Such as this man.

His hair was slicked back with what must have been way more than a coin-sized amount of gel, and he was extraordinarily sweaty. While his soul patch was, well . . . unfortunately visible, it didn't seem like it would be enough to keep his chin warm in this late autumn weather. Over his shoulder, he wore a bright blue backpack, scuffed around the edges but apparently keeping whatever contents it held in place.

He strode away from the gaming table. I stepped back for every step he took forward until he had unfortunately backed me into a corner.

"That's very kind of you, but I don't have time for a break. As you can see, we're a bit understaffed—" Sophie frowned, and I mouthed an apology at her. "And anyways, I can get coffees for fr—"

He held up his finger, stopping me in the middle of my sentence. "Got it. I'll bring the coffee to you, okay? You're not going to turn down some sweet, sweet caffeine, are you?"

"I'm not interested in any more caffeine today." When his face fell, I backtracked. "But I'm happy to help you if you have any questions about the shop or—"

"My name's Clive." He held out his hand. "Clive Newton. You may have heard of me. I'm a collector. Good friend of your dad's, actually."

I narrowed my eyes as I shook his hand, which was damp. Dad had been talking about "some big-headed collector" who kept trying to pawn off his junk to the store. I'd thought Dad had said "Chive" at the time and thought to myself, "Well, that's a funny name, Chive. What's his brother's name, Dill? Hope I never run into him."

Unfortunately, I now had. If only Dad had been in the shop today. I was no good at letting people know they were unwelcome and, even though I'd been back since the beginning of the semester, Of Dice and Decks still didn't feel as if it were mine.

I crossed my arms. "If you're here to sell, I'm afraid we're taking an indefinite hiatus from trade-ins."

I must have raised my voice a little too much, because one of our regulars—a graphic designer named Leon who used our gaming tables as a workspace every so often—glanced up from his tablet. When I noticed, he ducked with his cheeks flushed.

I lowered my voice. Yelling at customers did not a happy board game shop make, and we couldn't afford to lose regulars over someone who made outstaying their welcome a recreational sport. "My dad's got some medical bills coming up. It's just not a good time, okay?"

That was an understatement, but I tried to minimize as much as possible when talking about our somewhat lackluster finances. Sugar House had very little space for new businesses to move in. Buildings were coveted. Vultures liked to circle, if you got my meaning.

"Then you'll really want to see this. These will pay for whatever bills your dad has, and then some."

I pressed the bridge of my nose, exhaling slowly. I didn't like dealing with collectors. They tended to treat the person they're wanting to sell things to like they were stupid, and for very little money on the line. Our own shop had very few collectibles for sale and none of them worth more than a hundred dollars or so.

"Just a peek," persuaded Clive. "I get that you're closed to trades, but wouldn't you be kicking yourself if you found out just what I'm offering and you passed it up?"

Internally, I did a little mental math. What would be the faster way to get rid of him: argue with him about whatever twenty-dollar "gaming heirloom" he'd found in his grandma's attic and was now trying to foist upon us? Or let him show me, say "hmm, no thanks," and send him on his way?

It was a toss-up, but something told me I'd have better luck with this particular customer if I chose the latter. God help me.

Sighing, I gestured to the staff door past the gaming tables. "All right, follow me. We tend to do appraisals in the staff room, to keep from distracting the other customers with business talk."

The storage room was where we put old board games, the worn ones people returned or the ones that never sold. One time when I was twelve, a friend had traded me one of his Pokemon cards for a virtual Tamagotchi pet, so it wasn't a terrible stretch to say we conducted appraisals there, too.

It was also technically a break room. Technically, in that it had two metal fold-up chairs in the back corner. Though you try relaxing when you risk a board game avalanche killing you with every breath. It's an art that I'd never perfected, because I knew that when it came down to it, a misplaced game of Twilight Imperium could easily take me out.

I opened the door and weaved my way through the shelves of board games sticking out in every direction that a board game could, with Clive cursing under his breath a few feet behind me.

Somehow, we made it to the very back using similar techniques to hikers scaling a cliffside trail, and I only had to pull Clive away from a precarious stack of games twice. Only one hit him, but it was a small one, and, surprisingly, neither of us mentioned it.

There were two chairs in the same spot that they'd always been since I was at least four—facing each other, topped with even more board games that we had to push out of the way.

"Dang," muttered Clive. "Finances are worse than even I imagined, huh?"

I gritted my teeth. "We get by."

"Do you?" Clive coughed as some of the ceiling dust settled in the air. "Without getting asbestos poisoning, I mean?"

"The shop doesn't have any asbestos! We had it tested."

. . . anymore. It was an old building. I didn't want to get into it with Clive, though. I already spent enough of my childhood being lectured by Dad to be very diligent about physical exams, just in case the shop's renovations in the eighties hadn't gotten rid of everything.

"Like I said, we're not taking exchanges right now. We're trying to focus on what inventory we have."

"Sure, sure," said Clive, rummaging around in his backpack and blissfully ignoring the hint I'd tried to give him. "Sometimes, I think people don't know what they want until someone lays it out for them. Then they realize how wrong they were. Don't you?"

I thought about it for longer than such a question deserved, in case I was missing something.

"No, not really," I said. "That sounds like a pretty scummy moral philosophy."

"Potato, potato, Ben."

"You just pronounced it the same twice. That's not how that saying goes."

"I suppose you've heard," Clive continued, "of the beloved family relationship wrecker Monopoly?"

I groaned. Of course it had to do with some obscure variation of Monopoly. It always did.

"Let me guess. You have a rare . . . let's say, 2011 copy of Salt Lake City-opoly? That I could purchase for five dollars and some change at any thrift shop in the county?"

"Oh, please, don't insult me. You think I'm some kinda amateur? What I've got is worth even more than the 1985 Mormon-opoly with the infamous rule that makes you give ten percent of your earnings to church tithing."

A hundred-dollar gag gift from any online auctioneer worth their salt—not bad, but certainly nothing to get worked up about. And even then, I knew few collectors who would buy it so much as snort at its mention and ignore any eBay listings for it because it was horribly unplayable.

"I don't want to be rude," I said, "but if I wanted to play Guess Who, I'd pull out a copy."

"Snarky when you want to be. You really are Mr. Rosencrantz's son."

He smirked and pulled out the board game he'd been keeping in his backpack, which was padded with cotton balls to the brim, from what I could tell. Whatever was in there, he apparently cared enough to protect it—or to convince me that he did.

From out of there, he placed the board game case on the desk. It took me a few seconds to glean what I was looking at.

At first, it looked like a beat-up copy of Monopoly. Nothing too special about that, though you could get some that sold for a few thousand if they were from the early twentieth century or a solid gold one that would likely sell for much more if you a) stole from the Museum of American Finance and b) found a buyer willing to look the other way.

But then I frowned.

The title's font and the color scheme did not match earlier editions of Monopoly—the reds and greens more muted and formal than the more colorful and child-friendly design of the latter. There was a silhouette of an older woman where the Monopoly mascot, Uncle Pennybags, would be. But the crux was the title. It said, in big letters, THE LANDLORD'S GAME.

"How much do you know about Monopoly's history?" said Clive.

It took me a few seconds to answer. Not out of awe, necessarily, but to recall the information from whatever crevice in my brain it lived in.

"Enough to know the idea was more or less stolen from a woman named Lizzie Magie," I said, "who popularized a very similar game at the turn of the century."

The Landlord's Game was similar to Monopoly in terms of rules except in message. Even more notable, The Landlord's Game preceded it. The purpose of the game, according to its inventor, was to teach children how corporate monopolies destroyed the markets and communities they grew out of.

Of course, when the Parker Brothers co-opted the game with an opposite message, it was much more popular. Ironically, from what I understood, Lizzie Magie got none of the profits once the game she created found a larger audience. So much for her message, though if you asked me, she may have proven it in the most unfortunate way possible.

"You're good. Did your dad make you learn about all the old board game lore?"

I snorted. "No. I read about it in an Uncle John's bathroom reader. As I said, we prefer not to deal with collectibles. Whatever you're taking for this, I can guarantee you we can't afford it. It's probably worth more than what I'd make in a year."

"It is," promised Clive. "In this condition? If you can get it verified, this will fetch you sixty grand easy. One hundred grand if you can garner enough excitement among collectors."

That . . . I had not expected. Admittedly, my heart did race a little. I fantasized putting it up for bidding. Maybe we could even have a fundraiser. A silent auction, maybe to raise money for Dad's medical bills and run the shop in a less hectic state than we currently did.

"It's authentic?"

"Oh, yes. I've got some other games that might spark your interest, and I can direct you to my eBay listings if you'd like to peruse those," he continued, patting the game's cover harder than one should for something of that value. "But I can guarantee you this one's worth more than your entire inventory in cash."

If anything, that showed how little Clive understood about store inventory. Tempting, though, regardless of its inaccuracy.

But, while wishing I could bite my tongue and take the cash, I shook my head. "I'm sorry. We really don't have that sort of money."

"I'll take ten grand for the game. You could get a loan for that much, couldn't you?"

Ten grand was an insulting amount of money to accept for a game that was supposedly so valuable. You'd have to be insane, or at least desperate as all get-out, to sell it for that little. Something about his eyes—how much they blinked, maybe—made me scrutinize him. I hadn't begun the conversation with much trust for the man, but whatever I had, it fizzled out.

"Why are you so eager to pawn it off?"

He scrutinized me right back. If one of us was going to back down, it wasn't going to be him.

"That . . ." He chose his words carefully, in a way that made me feel like he was determining how much effort I was worth. "Is none of your business."

Ah, as I suspected. I rolled my eyes. As much as I really wanted to get embroiled in whatever low-level crimes this guy spent his day doing, well . . . I didn't. If I wanted less free time, I'd take up a hobby—and I'd suggest Clive do the same.

I pointed at the storage room door with my thumb. "Then you can take your business elsewhere."

"Did I mention that it's a first edition?"

I knew enough about collectible games to know a first edition was worth paying attention to for most any successful game. That would make it much closer to a six-figure value, especially if all the pieces were intact. I resisted the urge to check, though, in case Clive would try to pull some "you touch it, you buy it" nonsense or claim I broke a figurine.

Okay. So maybe this was nearing a Van Gogh–level price. One of his cheaper paintings. Not the ones with the sunflowers, definitely not, but valuable.

Yet apparently not to Clive.

"If you want the money that bad, why don't you auction it off yourself?" I asked.

"You know what, Mr. Rosencrantz?"

"Doctor, actually," I interrupted. Normally I didn't correct people, but this guy was getting on my nerves.

"Oh, I'm so sorry, doctor." He gave me a look. "You ask too many questions. It's not like you can afford to pass on this. I know how expensive rent gets, how much more the price rises year after year. In Sugar House? Please. You'll be out of business in . . ."

He sucked in through his teeth, like he really was considering. I could feel my face heating up, and it took all of my self-control not to bring out a variety of four-letter words on the tip of my tongue. Thankfully, being raised in Utah meant that I tended to break out a *darn* or, in dire circumstances, a *heck* at my most frustrated.

"Four months? Five if you sell all of your pants except, like, a patchy pair of corduroys?"

That . . . was way too specific. I rubbed my hands against my corduroys. If Frog and Toad could pull them off, I saw no reason why I couldn't. Now, Clive was just being rude for rudeness' sake.

"Look, we have other customers. I don't know where you got that, but I'm not discussing trades with you like this, all backway alley and 'Psst, kid, wanna buy a vintage game?' "

"Hey, you're the one who wanted to take this back here. There were barely any customers in your shop. I'd have been happy to discuss out in the open."

That was true, but during the day, our shop tended to be slow. The patrons who hung around in the gaming room got enough use out of the rental games, but half of them ended up buying them online after they left. I couldn't even blame them for it. I wasn't the only one who struggled to pay their bills in this city, and I couldn't compete with corporate prices.

I shook my head. I had better things to do than grapple with Clive, let alone air out feelings that he had no business barging into. Anything would be a better use of my time. I stood up and stormed out of the room—or as close as one could get to storming while gingerly navigating the storage room's haphazard organization.

Clive packed up his game quickly, then hurried out the door after me, and, miraculously, no board game stacks fell over after him. "Your choice! Close down in a few months, see if I care! Give it a year, and Sugar House won't remember your shop existed at all."

"That's enough. I'm sorry, Clive, but you don't get to come in here and discuss financial issues that you know nothing about." I motioned him towards the front door, something I should have done as soon as he stepped in. "If you're going to buy something or play games, you're welcome to stay. Otherwise, have a good day. You're welcome to come back as a customer, but if you return to discuss the game again, it'll be a waste of both of our time."

For a second, his eyes flashed. With rage? Fear? I couldn't

tell. But he stood up and headed for the door, hiding his scowl as best as he could.

"You won't," he said, sauntering off, "when you have to fend for yourself in the unemployment line."

"Won't what?"

He raised an eyebrow, hand on the door. "Have a good day."

"Ah, right."

I watched him leave the store, and I could feel my hands clenching as the little bell on top of the door jingled. It took an actual effort to unclench them. Few things could get me worked up to anger. I didn't like it, nor him, at all.

Leon put his tablet in his messenger bag and hurried to the front room.

"Are you guys really that close to closing?" he said, and I noticed the waver in his voice.

I shook my head, fully aware of how unconvincing I must have been but trying anyways.

"We'll survive. Dad kept the shop open for thirty years. I intend to keep it open for at least thirty more."

It was . . . an exaggeration, in some ways. I intended to keep it open as long as I could financially manage to, knowing it would break Dad's heart if it closed. But 2053 was quite a ways away and a lot to promise when I'd thought my marriage would last much longer than that. And, well.

"You have a whole gaming community rallying around you, you know. Everyone loves you guys." I didn't know if I believed that, but he said it with such conviction that I frowned a little less. "If there's anything I can do, let me know. I don't know where I'd be without your shop."

The thought of Leon, barely in his twenties and fending to make his own ends meet, doing what he could to help, cooled down the flames of irritation Clive's visit had left me with. It was a kind gesture, but one I'd never dream of taking him up on. Surely he had heavier things to worry about than a dusty old shop.

"What do you know about that man—Clive?" I asked Leon. "I've heard my dad talk about him, but this is the first I've seen of him."

Leon took his time to respond, his eyebrows knit. "He's . . . unpleasant. But he has connections to a lot of rich nerds in Utah, and that gives you a reputation if you're a collector."

"A good reputation?" When Leon didn't answer, I prodded just a little further. "What do you mean? Do you trust him?"

Now a quick response—he couldn't shake his head harder without getting whiplash. "No! He's the sketchiest guy I know. Whatever you do, don't buy anything from him. And don't trust anything he says."

"Those were the vibes I got," I said. "I'm glad to have them confirmed."

I thanked Leon, asked Sophie to watch the cash register for me, and spent an embarrassingly long time in the bathroom with my head in my hands. I didn't cry. I was too tired for that. And anyways, I'd cried enough this year that the effort just wasn't there anymore. There was only so much crying you could do before the tears went away, yet the heaviness in your chest remained.

When I returned, Sophie was shooing me out the door like I'd done to Clive just moments ago.

"It's almost noon, Ben. Don't you have a date to attend to?"

"A date?"

I'd almost forgotten. Uncomfortable social interactions always flustered me, and Clive had been enough discomfort to fill my quota for the decade.

"Yes, I'd better get going." It was hardly a date, but she had a point that I needed to leave, and I had little time to argue. I couldn't be late. "What about you? I can't just leave you alone."

"Give it until one, and I bet your dad will be bored enough to come in and say hello, whether he feigns retirement or not." She shot me a half-smile. "And anyways, Tuesday afternoons are hardly our busy hours."

"That's implying," I said, "that we have busy hours at all."

Chapter 3

✤

With an overcoat slipped on and car keys, I hurried over to the shop next door: McCaslin's Flowers & Events. It was one of the newer stores on our street. From what I'd understood, the owner, Ezra McCaslin—a Southern Utah transplant who, despite the cold and the busier pace up north, had established himself as a fixture without too much trouble—had opened it just a few months before I'd moved back. The ground crunched unpleasantly with leaves and partially melted snow under my shoes. No matter. I would brave the potentially wet socks for an acquaintance in need.

Ezra's shop had first caught my eye for two reasons besides the fact that we were next-door neighbors, with only a dumpster's worth of separation between our two stores.

First, because it had taken the place of the old art gallery with the owner who used to shoo me out of her shop "before I knocked anything over" when I was growing up (though to her credit, I was a clumsy kid, and she was likely right to want me anywhere besides in her store).

Second, because I noticed his sign always said "free flowers if your name is [insert name here]," and usually ones that catered to Utah moms and their mystifying spelling conventions like Brynleigh or Dallinleigh . . . anything with -leigh, really. For the first week or so, I kept hoping the name Ben would appear as some sort of sign from the universe that I would be all right back in my hometown. Around the second week, Ezra came into Of Dice and Decks to say hello to me in person after hearing from Dad that I'd moved back home.

He left me with about fifty dollars' worth of flowers at no charge to myself, which then sat in Dad's dining room until they'd wilted and the petals fell to the floor, where my dog, Beans, sniffed at (but thankfully did not eat) them. Dad asked me if they were "from a special someone."

I asked him if he knew much about the new flower shop and its owner in particular, in part because I figured I should keep positive relations with the other local business owners. And because, while I had no interest in dating for the near future, I couldn't help but admit he was sweet.

"They're from Ezra, then?" He'd shaken his head, barely looking up from the thriller novel he'd picked up from the grocery store along with dinner. "Nice man. Just opened shop a few months ago. Hmm, you could do much worse."

I didn't ask him what he meant by that. It was better sometimes, with Dad, not to ask. Particularly when my love life (or lack thereof) was concerned.

Ezra's shop looked like many of the others in Sugar House from the outside. It had once been a Tudor-style home renovated into a shop to save space, which was hard to come by in Salt Lake City. Cobblestone steps led up to the entrance. Even as close to winter as it was, the light coming from the shop windows looked warm.

It was a loved little building. You could tell by the paint, chipped and revealing previous layers. That, of course, showed that someone cared enough to keep on painting it even though they knew it would chip away. He was lucky to have found it, and the building itself was lucky to have found someone who treated it with such care.

I opened the door, which set off a tinkling bell.

"Ezra?" I called.

I looked around the shop. Empty, besides of course the flowers. Though it was late in the season, Ezra grew enough with his greenhouse out back that he had a decent little variety on display. He tried, from what I understood, to grow as much as he could and source from nearby businesses where he couldn't.

I took a deep breath and sighed in contentment. Being in his shop awoke the Pavlovian part of me that needed a floral-scented sleep spray to drift off. A few whiffs of the flowers, and I almost forgot about Clive. And had a sudden craving for warm milk and a gummy melatonin. I ignored the latter part.

"Back door's open!" a voice said from, as one might expect, the back door.

Said door was ajar, so I took the liberty of stepping through. I'd never been in the back of Ezra's shop before. It was cluttered, but in a thoughtful way—ribbons in this box, and a line of vases on that shelf.

Ezra himself hovered over a workbench, though he straightened up when I came in.

"You made it!"

Ezra McCaslin was tall and wiry, and his apron hung a tad awkwardly off his lanky body, exposing one of the many band T-shirts he wore underneath it—which fit him, as he bore a passing resemblance to Gerard Way. His hair, brown and curly, was pulled up in a blue scrunchie, though some strands had escaped the ponytail and hung down in his face as he pored over a flower arrangement that I could only describe as *autumnal* and *complicated*.

I handed him the car keys. "Sorry for the delay. We had a difficult . . ."

I paused for a minute, thinking of how one might sum up Clive in a way that didn't involve continuous screaming. I shuddered. Not possible.

"It doesn't matter," I finished. "You should have enough gas to last the night. I don't tend to drive much during the snowy months."

"You have no idea how thoroughly you're saving my life right now, Ben." He shoved the keys in his pocket and clapped my back in a half-hug. "Of course the Trooper would die out on me today!"

This, as I had learned this morning when Ezra burst into Of Dice and Decks in a panic, was a 1985 Isuzu Trooper that had somehow remained Ezra's main source of transportation since his great-aunt had sold it to him in high school for a Cosmic Brownie and some pocket change. Or it had been until Ezra'd left the light on the night before and no number of frantic jump-starts would save it.

When he'd taken it to the mechanic, Ezra had explained, all they did was laugh and laugh and suggest that he look into auto loans. Fifteen years with the vehicle, and he couldn't even sell the Trooper to earn back that brownie-and-some-change investment.

Since it was so unexpected and left him with no time to find a rental before making his flower deliveries, I was letting him borrow my car for the day.

"I'm sorry for your loss," I said.

"It leaked exhaust in the cabin, and sometimes the passenger door would open on the highway, but I'm still going to miss it," he said sadly.

"What a rich life. For a car, I mean. What time is the wedding at, again?"

"Not until seven, so I've got plenty of time," he said. "I just want to take a look, make sure I have the arrangements ready to, uh . . . mask the presence of other surroundings."

"Other surroundings?"

Ezra chuckled nervously. "The bride is a professor of marine life, so naturally, she chose her wedding location at . . ."

He trailed off, giving me a meaningful look.

"Oh, no," I said. "Not the aquarium."

"Right out front," he said. "Underneath The Claw."

Indoors, the Salt Lake County aquarium was much like any

other. Cute, even. There were sharks, octopi, even penguins. Normal aquarium fare. It was friendly. It was *educational.*

But outside was a piece of two-hundred-foot-tall octopus-themed concert equipment that the city had added out front to "draw in visitors." Though it didn't look much like an octopus. It looked like an oversized skill crane claw that had escaped from the mall and planted itself right by the highway, where people could see and get into multi-car pile-ups because of it.

They called it The Claw.

It was an eyesore at its most benign and had been around long enough to practically be counted as a local cryptid. The closest Salt Lake City had to one, anyways, though I'd have preferred a Bigfoot or two. I wouldn't put it past it to be a cause of unexplained headaches, crop circles, and the like. As it was, I blamed it for at least half of my problems.

"Isn't it too cold for an outdoor wedding?"

"They said they don't care. They're placing heaters out and advising their guests to dress warm."

"I'll pray for you," I said.

"You and my neighbors both," he muttered under his breath. "All right if I return it this evening? Let's say sixish?"

"Of course. Just drop it off out front of the shop when you're done. You'll be at the business owners' meeting tonight, right?"

"I will indeed! Maybe if the happy couple loves the flowers enough, I can sneak you back some hors d'oeuvres. Think of it as a birthday present. Big three-oh today, right?"

I rolled my eyes. "You got me. Are you going to check my ID next?"

It wouldn't be the first time. In my early days of teaching, some of my new colleagues would ask me if I was lost and looking for the dorms when they first met me. These days, I'd felt like I'd finally grown into looking my age.

Which was a relief for me. It was a hit to my ego sometimes to have my hairstylist asking me what I was majoring in at college when I was the one teaching it. Even worse when, just as I'd open the syllabus to start the first course of a semester, a freshman would raise their hand and ask me if I knew when the teacher would arrive.

"I did have something for you." Ezra disappeared under the table and reappeared with a bouquet of sunflowers. "Think of it as somewhere between a thank-you and an actual birthday present."

"Do you give all of your customers flowers to say thanks?" I said, in a softer voice than I'd meant to.

I was still getting used to being the recipient of flowers again. That was all. Even platonic flowers (I presumed) got me flustered. Not that my ex-husband Shane had bought me much in the way of small gifts. We'd spent much of our marriage ignoring the gravity of our commitment to each other and wondering separately if we'd made the right decision.

Apparently not.

He waved me off. "Just the ones I like, especially the ones that blush when I hand it to them."

I wasn't looking to date, not any time soon. But whenever Ezra flirted with me, I couldn't help but hate Shane just a little for the hurt I felt whenever I considered the vulnerability that came with romance. It would be too much, I thought, to open myself to someone in that way again.

But I'd be lying if I said I didn't miss it. After years with someone, it's hard to adjust to being alone again.

"I'm lucky you like them, anyways. With how generous you've been, I should technically owe you a life debt. Or dinner, at least."

"Small businesses have to stick together, don't they?"

He grinned. "I can't argue with that. I'll be there tonight, Ben. Do I need to bring any games? I prefer the video variety, but I might have a copy of Yahtzee in the back of the Trooper. Been meaning to donate it to a thrift store for two, three years? I could finally put it to good use."

"No, they tend to play one specific game at that meeting. Have you heard of Nertz?"

He had not, and I tried as best as I could to explain the rules to him as he packed up his wedding decorations. It had been a while since my own wedding, which had been less, shall we say, memorable in location than The Claw. But the flowers gave a splash of color that would be hard to find this close to winter in Utah, and with a decorator as thoughtful as Ezra on their side, I had no doubts that the couple's day would be meaningful.

As I helped him carry the wedding flowers to my car (an unremarkable Ford Fusion, which I'd named "Fjord") and reassured him that all he need bring to the local business owners' meeting was himself, he added, "I guess what my friends back home said about Northern Utahns was right. You guys *are* so nice."

I winced, though he couldn't see it behind the box of flowers. "We certainly can be." And we could be a lot of other things, too. Busy, terrible drivers, and judgmental towards anyone who didn't fit the norm, among other things. But I didn't want to dampen the mood.

"You said they play Nertz?"

"Yes. It's a bit of an obscure choice, maybe, but it's as I said. If you know Solitaire—"

"Solitaire was the only game on my mom's laptop growing up. I know that too well."

"Excellent. Then you'll catch on quickly," I said.

"Maybe if I make it on the earlier side of six," he said, "we could play a few warm-up rounds?"

"Of course."

Even if I couldn't fathom being in a relationship right now, maybe Ezra and I could still be friends. Sooner or later, he'd find someone less broken than me. Someone who could appreciate him without crushing him with all their baggage. In the meantime, we could keep each other company.

Chapter 4

❧

Exiting Ezra's flower shop, I found myself face-to-face with an unwelcome sight. One that I'd just gotten myself away from an hour earlier. Clive strode up the street, maybe one hundred feet away. And he walked fast, purposeful.

I weighed the possibility of doing a one-eighty back into Ezra's shop. What would be more socially acceptable? Maybe, I thought to myself as I hunched my shoulders and looked down, I could get through this without him noticing me.

As he approached, I realized he wasn't looking at me. He didn't seem to notice me at all. His cell phone was pressed in between his shoulder and his ear, and he was speed-walking so quickly that it was quite the effort just for him to hold it in place. His face was even more flushed than it was earlier, and it was twisted into something near rage.

"Of course I've got it! You think I'd just pawn it off on any idiot?" He scoffed, which seemed to leave him winded, and shoved his other hand in his blazer pocket. "Look—I'll meet you, I will, but you've got to promise me you won't flake out this time."

As he passed me, he nearly shoved me off the sidewalk. Not out of any purposeful malice, it seemed. It was just that I was a roadblock to wherever he needed to go.

That caught his attention, and he lifted his mouth away

from the receiver. He scrutinized me, opened his mouth as if to say something (a four-letter something, I'd assume), then rolled his eyes and stalked back down the sidewalk.

"But you've got to make it worth my while, okay? I'm not going down on my price this time, and I don't think you'll find anyone else who has what I've got."

Still about that game, then. I wondered if I were the idiot he'd "never pawn something so special and rare" off on. Then, I figured that when it came to people like Clive, sometimes it's good not to be admired.

Leon exited Of Dice and Decks' front door. I balked, praying to whoever took it upon themselves to listen that he hadn't seen Clive nearly push me into the street.

He gave me a thumbs-up, eyebrows raised in a silent question.

Damn it. Clearly he had noticed the interaction. Normally Leon was a chill, mind-his-own-business kind of guy. Clive must have set off alarms in his head that got through his chill exterior.

I mirrored his thumbs-up and let go of what little shreds of dignity I had to spare.

When I returned to the shop, I kept hold of the flowers until Sophie pointed them out.

"Ezra said they're an early birthday present," I said absently. "Sorry, I'd forgotten I was holding them. They're nice, aren't they?"

Sophie nodded, resting her chin against her hand. "When's the wedding?"

I looked up sharply. If I'd been drinking something, I would have spat it. "Our what?"

Sophie smirked. "Not your wedding, Ben. The one he's decorating. Didn't you say that's why he needed your keys?"

I relaxed, thankful none of the few customers in the shop

seemed to be listening to our conversation. "Sometime tonight, I think, though he needs to set up much earlier. He's
heading out right now."

I placed them on the desk next to the register, which
mainly held Dad's knickknacks—a photo of him and me at a
local comic convention fifteen-odd years ago; a bobblehead
of the Incredible Hulk.

The Hulk seemed to nod at them in approval. Considering
that the bobblehead was so old that I could barely get it to do
that on purpose, I took it as an auspicious sign. Who was I to
pretend I knew better than Bobble Hulk?

For the rest of the afternoon, I tried to forget Clive's phone
call—and not just because I was pretty sure some of it insulted me. Friday nights were busy at Of Dice and Decks.
Four of our five gaming tables were rented out—two group
date nights, a tabletop roleplaying campaign, and the bi-
weekly small business owners' meeting for shops on our
street.

It was a meeting in name that had devolved into a Nertz
tournament. Nertz was a card game that involved one deck
per person, similar in rules to Solitaire if it involved more
yelling. Once, the meeting had simply been to discuss business and any issues one owner had with another. But most of
the time, the businesses in Sugar House got along well
enough. And so, as I've heard it told, Dad challenged the
group there to a game of Nertz to pass the time.

Now, it wasn't a proper meeting without it.

Not one to miss a game of Nertz, Dad indeed came in
around five-thirty to "man the cashier's station while I got
the meeting set up." He watched me run back and forth from
the kitchen to the gaming room for the better part of an hour,
occasionally giving customers his advice on which games
they'd enjoy.

"You've seen us play Nertz often enough. Would you say

you understand the rules?" He waited for me to nod. "I'd like you to borrow something for me tonight."

From the cashier's desk, he grabbed a worn, squarish object and put it in my hand.

It was his special deck of playing cards, specifically for beating other small business owners in Nertz. The large-print font and minimalistic design, he explained, made it perfect for playing. They were unassuming yet distinct in a bold color that, if I were a crayon namer, I might have called something like "Victory Violet."

"Nothing like Kit's deck," sniffed Dad once, when I made the mistake of asking why it was so good. "Kit uses a *Star Wars* Villains deck. Terrible color scheme. Unreadable. I hate their deck."

Kit Leavitt ran the Devil's Brewery, a pub several blocks away. They held slam poetry nights on the weekends where I had thoroughly embarrassed myself performing passionate (if not the best or even soberly written) love poems when I'd come home from college over the summer.

But to Dad, Kit was the only Nertz player who came even a little close to beating him. They sometimes lost rounds of Nertz but, in the twenty years I'd known them, I'd never seen them lose a game to anyone but Dad. And even then, the record heavily leaned towards Kit. A tender spot on Dad's ego. He must have felt that, as the owner of a board game shop, he had something to prove.

But Kit had something better: fast reflexes.

"I can't take these," I said. "You've seen me play. I'll make a disgrace of your reputation."

"Just don't bet any money and you'll be fine." Dad frowned, then added, "And don't sample any of Kit's wares until you're done playing."

"Can't make any promises," I said.

Though I had no plans of drinking tonight. I'd had a confusing enough day as it was without adding beer to the mix. And besides, if I were to take Dad's place in the Nertz competition, drinking wouldn't exactly help me.

"Are you feeling okay today?"

"Okay?" he repeated, nonplussed.

"It's just . . . I've never known you to turn down a game of Nertz."

"I'm *all right*, Ben," Dad insisted, in the voice he often used when he wanted someone to drop the subject. Usually he employed it when discussions about the best edition of Dungeons & Dragons went awry, or if someone asked him why we didn't renovate the café into a soda shop, and did we know that soda shops were very profitable here in Utah, actually? We did know that, but they failed to take into consideration that we did not care.

"Besides," he added. "This will be Ezra's first meeting. He might feel more comfortable with you there."

I rolled my eyes. While Dad's interest in my love life was, if not appreciated, at least tolerated, something told me that pursuing the store owner next door was a little risky. If we broke up, it's not like one of us could just pack up shop and move somewhere else. It wasn't practical.

At around seven, Sophie and I set up two of the back tables for the business owners' meeting, even though her shift was almost up, and the evening barista—a fancy title I gave myself for the less glamorous task of having to run two jobs—would have to take over her work.

We arranged the tables in a shape that offered enough room for cards, drinks, and (most importantly) snacks. I set a bowl out of all the main junk food groups—pretzels, cheesy chips, and even peach rings. And napkins, of course, to keep anyone from getting snack dust all over the cards. Board game enthusiasts loved a good game night snack, but nobody wanted their cards to get grimy.

"It's like charcuterie for goblins," I said, clasping my hands together when the spread was finished.

The first person to show up was Kit, hastily taking off their name tag as they walked in and unloading a six-pack of sours on one of the tables. For those who didn't drink or appreciate an evening caffeine buzz, a selection of the café's herbal teas were available.

"Busy night?"

Kit chuckled under their breath. "Let's just say my poor evening manager is running on four hours of sleep and the grace of God this shift. But I'm here, and I've got two good hours in me before I need to go back and help 'em close."

"Do you think it'll affect your game?"

Kit looked down at me, their green eyes sparkling. "Your dad mentioned up front that it's your first time playing with us. Do you know what that means, kiddo?"

"What?" I asked, ignoring the fact that no one besides Kit had called me *kiddo* in at least a decade, and I preferred it that way.

"That if I were you, I'd worry about yourself."

"Right," I said weakly, half a mind to ask Dad if he wanted to play after all.

Next to arrive was Leon, an honorary member since he ran his budding graphic design business from the gaming tables at least two days out of every given week. According to him, the coffee was cheaper here and the rates much better than a coworking space. He handed me three crumpled-up twenty-dollar bills.

"What's this?"

"It's my turn to cover the tables," he said. "Keep the change."

He said that last part meaningfully, and I groaned, remembering Clive's conversation with me earlier today. The last thing I needed was customers aware of our financial troubles. They were much more likely to overreact about it, and we were still far from closing our doors altogether.

"That really isn't necessary, Leon," I said. "I promise the shop's not going under anytime soon. Use the change to buy yourself dinner."

"I don't want dinner," he insisted. "I want to put in a donation."

"Even if the shop was about to go under," Kit said, "do you think a few extra dollars would make a difference?"

Leon shrugged, blushing. There was an uncomfortable, seconds-long silence.

"You could consider it a birthday present," he said falteringly. "You're thirty-five today, right?"

"Just thirty. But thanks." Finally, I rubbed my temples. "All right, but let's not call it a present. How about we count it as a head start for whoever foots the next meeting. We really don't need the extra help. All right?"

Extra help would have been welcome in most other situations, such as from the bank. But it didn't feel right to mooch off Leon. I didn't know much about what freelance graphic designers made, but I'm sure it wasn't enough to just burn money for the sake of it.

Besides, Kit was right. Our rent was quite a bit more than a few dollars.

Dr. Petras and her wife Yael came in next, setting a box of orange rolls next to Kit's beer.

I waved as they both sat down. "Hello, Dr. Petras! How's your granddaughter liking Rummikub?"

"Are you still calling her that, Ben?" Yael turned to her wife. "He knows you have a first name, doesn't he?"

I rocked back on my feet nervously. "Sorry, old habits."

"To answer your question, she's catching on too quickly," said Dr. Petras, shaking her head. "Almost beat me last night, and I stopped going easy on her several games ago."

Yael squeezed Dr. Petras's hand. "You can't make me feel

bad for either of you. They pulverize my score every time, and I *am* going hard on them."

"Perhaps tonight's the night you'll win at Nertz," I suggested, to which she laughed so hard she snorted.

"I don't mean to offend you," she said, "but the best I can hope for is coming second-to-last. Nertz is even more unforgiving."

"Second-to-last?" I said, then understood. "Oh. Right. If you want, I could ask Dad if he'd prefer to—"

"No!" said everyone, almost at once.

"We like your dad, Ben," Kit said. "And we appreciate him letting us use the store to meet. But the rest of us are excited to have a damn chance for once."

Dad, manning the storefront, poked his head through the cracked door. "My hearing's fine, thanks."

"Love you, Martin!" called Dr. Petras.

Stoic, Dad nevertheless gave her a thumbs-up. "It's Mr. Rosencrantz to anyone but you, Britt."

The second-to-last one was Quentin Lang, one of Dad's college buddies who ran a European food market in between Kit's brewery and Dr. Petras and Yael's cinnamon roll delivery shop. He and a few other members of their fraternity had been some of the original Dungeons & Dragons players back in the eighties when it was just getting started. Which, since this was Utah and there was initially a huge "Satanic Panic" around it, was impressive. Growing up, I'd watch and later play campaigns with him and Dad. He nearly always played a wizard, and his knowledge of the D&D Spellbook was formidable.

As were his Nertz skills. He wasn't quite at the same speed level as Dad or Kit, but he was strong enough of a player that I had no delusions of beating him. After all, he and Dad had plenty of head-to-head Nertz battles when they were roommates. As he took out his deck of cards, he sized Dad's own deck that I'd set on the table.

"Before you ask," I said nervously, "I know I'm not as good as my dad, but I'm giving it my best shot."

Quentin bit his lip, but he couldn't help the grin spreading on his face. "Just don't bend the cards, okay, Ben?"

For now, it was just the five of us—six, counting Ezra, who came in a few moments later. He was wearing a button-down flannel that I don't think he'd been wearing earlier, and he had let his hair down out of its ponytail. When he sat down, I smelled cologne or some sort of perfume—cinnamon-apple, maybe? Had he worn it to freshen himself up a little bit for this?

Probably not. Where would he have found the time? But he looked nice nonetheless.

"Sorry," he said, taking his place at the table. "I was hoping we would have time to practice before, Ben."

Dr. Petras looked between him and me. She didn't say anything, but a small smirk lit up her face.

"You run the flower shop next door, don't you?" Dr. Petras's glasses glinted in the light, which was unnerving. "Well, I hope you're as good at Nertz as you are flower arrangement. None of us are here to go easy on you."

It could be said that, at times, this group took games a bit too seriously. Board game enthusiasts, as you can imagine, like games best when they are winning. Sometimes that led to shocking competitiveness. Hurt feelings rarely mani-fested themselves outside of the gaming table, but . . . the words people said when they were losing weren't always kind. Or PG.

I shook my head at Dr. Petras as if to say, "Please don't make this a bigger deal than it needs to be." She'd meddled enough in my love life through high school. At thirty, I wanted that facet to be left alone. Maybe forever.

But if they noticed, they ignored it.

"I'll do my best." Ezra didn't appear fazed by Dr. Petras. If anything, he seemed delighted. "I haven't played Nertz, but I've been told I'm pretty good at Uno as long as no pile-ons of plus-fours head my way."

A horrible vision of this group attempting to play Uno entered my head. I shuddered. Piles of plus-fours, indeed.

"You don't play much, then?" said Quentin, looking at Ezra like a hungry shark who smelled some poor baby seal with a nosebleed not too far away.

"No." I was surprised that Ezra did not seem intimidated at all. "I'm more into video games, actually. But I'd love to learn."

For a second, I thought all of the small business owners' crew were going to turn full-on snob and trash-talk Ezra out of the room. But that didn't happen. Most of them were, well, more or less polite about it.

"I love Tetris," offered Dr. Petras. "A little too much, actually. Sometimes I 'call in sick' to my office hours because I had a bad round with it and want to sulk."

"I've made so many farms on Stardew Valley," added Kit, "that sometimes I wake up in a panic thinking I need to water my plants. And I live in a studio apartment above the brewery. All I have up there is a potted cactus and some long-dead basil."

Even Quentin begrudgingly admitted that he spent most of his undergrad years at an arcade trying to beat their Donkey Kong high score (though he only ever got to third place). Likely with Dad, if I were to guess. The two had a knack for platforming games, and they both used it to destroy me in Super Smash Brothers.

Ezra sat down across the table from me, looking fairly pleased with himself. I knew that feeling. I had felt it, too, when I'd first returned home. It's nice to feel as though you belong someplace. Besides people like Clive, who tried to take advantage of it, Of Dice and Decks was for everyone.

"Any real business to discuss?" said Dr. Petras. "If so, we're gonna need to get Martin in here or at least have Ben take notes."

There were a few moments of silence, during which I patted my coat pocket for a pen. There were two. I never knew in my previous career when I'd need an ink pen.

Then, Dr. Petras grinned. "I thought not. Ezra, I hope you brought a deck of cards with you, because the ones available to borrow here are terribly unlucky. I should know. I've played with all of them. Shall we begin?"

Chapter 5

I finished in the Nertz game tournament with a respectable second-to-last behind Yael, who nearly threw a cinnamon roll at my head when I accidentally blocked her from unloading a run of threes. Ezra had come in between Leon and Dr. Petras, a promising score for his first time playing Nertz. If he played his cards right (*ba dum tss*), he might even be able to compete with my dad someday.

One of the first rules of Nertz is that while it is being played, there are no friends or alliances. There are only players who you'd better hope don't have faster reflexes than you. I'd always preferred cooperative games like Pandemic or Gloomhaven, where each player worked together for a collective win. And if you were to ask me, one of those types might be more productive for a business owners' meeting.

But Nertz was non-negotiable for the group, and so I kept my opinions to myself. After all, most of them besides Leon and Ezra had kept their businesses running for decades. Who was I to disrupt their routine?

After the last patrons left (and Dad, so he could let out my Chihuahua, Beans, while I closed), Ezra helped me clean up all the food wrappers and put the other board games in their usual spots on the shelves.

"I can help you close, if you want."

"You don't have to do that," I protested.

Ezra fought to keep from smiling. "I know that, Ben. But I want to."

I hesitated. "I'm not keeping you from anything, am I?"

Or anyone, I wanted to add. But even the thought of hinting at asking Ezra if he was single made my ears go hot. I'd practically stumbled into my last marriage out of shyness. Shane had always been the one to make the moves. It was nice, in some ways. Less to worry about, at least in the beginning.

"Just a cat," he said.

I perked up at this. Pets, I was much more comfortable with than people.

"What's his name?"

"Grandpa," said Ezra.

"Just Grandpa? Nothing else?"

"He doesn't need anything else. I adopted him . . ." He counted on his fingers. "Ten years ago? Eleven? And they thought he was a senior then. I almost wish he had a birth certificate so I could try and submit his age to Guinness World Records."

There was a brief, awkward silence. Then, I said, "Do you have any pictures of him?"

"Oh, yes. Too many, you might say. It's all I ever take pictures of." Ezra got his phone out of his pocket, then frowned. "Dang it. Phone's dead."

"Another time," I said. Then, to make conversation, "What did you think of your first meeting? They didn't scare you off from returning, did they?"

"Not as much actual housekeeping as I'd assumed, but far be it from me to complain about that. They're ruthless about that game, but I don't mind a challenge."

Ezra had come in fourth place, and I wasn't yet sure if that would earn the group's respect or mark him as a target for the next Nertz game. Probably both. But that was no bad thing, necessarily.

"Wait until you see my dad play," I said. "I think part of the reason it took me so long to learn is because he never went easy on me. Not even when I was a kid."

"Not so much a gentle nudge out of the nest as a shove?" When I nodded, he grinned. "I get that sense from him, at least when it comes to games."

Growing up, I'd never been deluded into thinking I was good at a game because Dad went easy on me. But, on the positive side, I at least knew when I'd really surpassed Dad's skills in a game.

"I can tell he missed you, though. And all of them, too."

Had they missed me? I'd certainly missed them. Teaching during the day kept me busy, but over the last year, I'd come home to an empty house every night. The hours stretched so painfully with no one to talk to besides the occasional friend's visit.

Having family and old friends around was nice. Not that I wouldn't miss my colleagues in Seattle, but I'd needed time back at home.

"What's it like, being back?"

I snapped out of my reverie. "To Salt Lake City?"

"Yeah. I guess I might move back to St. George someday, but I feel like if I go back, it wouldn't fit me anymore. Like either it will change or I will, or maybe both."

St. George was a town in Southern Utah, near the Nevada and Arizona borders. I'd only been a few times when I was younger, just passing through for a scouting trip. If Northern Utah was known for skiing, then Southern Utah was for mountain biking. Both parts of the state liked to say the other was full of themselves, with St. George close-minded and a decade behind on trends and Salt Lake City stuck-up and so fast-paced that living in it was like getting your shoelaces stuck in a treadmill.

But I imagined they were more alike than not. At least they had a passion for fry sauce and the insistence that Utah was the only place whose residents had ever mixed ketchup and mayonnaise (or, even more audacious, the first in all of history) to unify them.

"It does make sense, yeah. In some ways, it's different, but I think in better ways. There's less of a mold you're pressured to fit to belong than there was when I was younger."

Being one of two kids out at my high school didn't exactly make things easy on me. I hadn't grown up Mormon, but I understood enough about the surrounding culture to know that a) Mormon theology didn't involve a hell as such, and yet b) half of my classmates (and teachers, behind my back) believed I would be going to one someday. Even if they didn't say it to your face, the way they held you at a distance told you enough as a kid to know your invitation for more than one birthday party would get "lost in the mail."

"Oh, Salt Lake is miles better than St. George. Big cities are always more open-minded."

I chuckled without being able to help it. "Salt Lake City is big?"

It sounded pretentious as soon as I said it, but it was hard for me to see Salt Lake as big—even if it was the largest city in Utah. Maybe it was just because I grew up in it, but it had always seemed fairly small to me. Seattle was big, overwhelmingly so at times, but full of different possibilities than Salt Lake.

"Are you kidding?" said Ezra. "So much bigger. A boundless number of possibilities. I could even learn skiing, if I wanted to."

"Do you?"

He made a face. "It's a little cold, but maybe. If I was forced to. At gunpoint."

"Stunning praise. It wasn't the snow that brought you here, then?"

"The snow's what kept me away for so long, actually."

"If you don't mind me asking, what did?"

Ezra went quiet for a few moments as he swept.

"My mom's from here," he said finally. "She raised my sister and me, more or less on her own. After she passed away, and my sister Wren moved up here, there wasn't a ton keeping me there."

"I'm so sorry to hear that," I said quietly.

"It's okay, but it's not at the same time, you know?" He chuckled. "But it's been good, being up here. I feel closer to her than I have since I lost her."

"If I were to lose my dad . . ." I shook my head. "I can't imagine what that's like, but I'm so glad you've found comfort."

"It's better than staying in St. George. All the memories were there, but she wasn't anymore. If that makes sense."

"It does."

"Plus, there's much more I can grow here than in Southern Utah. It's not exactly habitable to plants, unless you like dead ones. During the less frozen months, that is. In the meantime, perfect weather for cuddling up and watching a movie."

I almost asked him what movies he liked, but the thought of what it might be like to cuddle him entered my mind. I cast it away, my face heating up, and soon I lost the train of thought.

"I bet your mom would be proud of you," I said. "It's hard opening your own shop. There were some nights growing up where we had to heat the bathwater on the stove because we couldn't pay the gas bill for a few days."

"Maybe," he said. "I dropped out of medical school to do it. Think she'd have been even more proud of me if I'd become a psychologist, but I knew I'd regret it if I did and then I actually had to work in the field."

"You wanted to be a psychologist?"

He grinned. "Strange, isn't it? I thought I did. That was

before residency, of course. The sessions kept getting to me. It got too hard to turn off my work thoughts at the end of the day. I got burned out, took a semester off, and never quite returned."

"You have a good heart."

"I don't know about that. If I had a stronger one, maybe I would have stayed." He scratched the back of his head. "Plus, the smell of the flowers relaxes me. I figure that even if people are buying them for a sad occasion, they might bring a little brightness into their life. I'm hoping, in that way, that I can still help people. Even if indirectly."

"The scent of all the different flowers is what I love most about your shop, too," I admitted.

"Is that so? Maybe I'll have to send you home with flowers more often," said Ezra. "In the meantime . . . I'm not sure if any restaurants are still open. But if you want, you're welcome at my apartment. I could make you dinner."

I'd dated around long enough before Shane to know what an invitation back to someone's apartment meant. Was it commitment? No. But it still implied a certain intimacy that I didn't know if I had the strength to give without crumbling. And though our divorce was finalized, I hadn't exactly redownloaded the old dating apps or anything like that.

And yet . . . Ezra was sweet. He made me smile, and he was one of the few people besides longtime friends I felt comfortable around after moving back. The anxiety I usually felt in social situations wasn't quite so sharp around him. I could talk, at least. It wasn't often that I found that.

Before I could respond (and how I would have, I didn't know), we were interrupted by a round of knocks in succession to the front door. Or more like thuds, really. But just coordinated enough that it sounded more like a person's hand than a bird colliding against a window, like I'd initially thought.

"The door's locked," I said. "And we're closed, anyway."

The knocks came again, this time louder and more desperate.

"Do you ever get after-hours customers?" Ezra suggested. "Game night emergencies?"

"No, I don't think we've had one of those since we held the midnight release of fifth-edition D&D. Almost ten years ago."

This time, the knocking didn't stop. Ezra and I exchanged glances.

"Well," said Ezra slowly. "Maybe you have one now."

"Or maybe an axe murderer has gone for the least stealthy method of attack." I shuddered, despite the sarcasm. "I guess I should answer it, though. I haven't gotten any texts from Dad, but maybe something happened."

In that case, I would have preferred the axe murderer. Dad had gone through enough lately.

"I'll stand right behind you," Ezra joked. "If it is a murderer, I'll grab the nearest copy of Risk and hit them over the head with it."

It wasn't until I'd cautiously removed the lock and swung the door open that he added, "Though if it were something with your dad, wouldn't he use his keys?"

In any case, I could tell even in the dim evening light that this was not Dad. That cheap blazer, I would recognize anywhere. Hours earlier, its owner had retreated, claiming I would regret the day I'd met him at all.

Clive Newton was standing at my door. Trembling, pale, and wordless.

Of course, the knife in his chest would account for his lack of speech.

I hardly processed that last part, though, before his eyes rolled up in the back of his head and he collapsed. The sound of his head hitting the metal railing outside our shop would echo in my head for days afterward.

But at the time, I could barely get out a stammered, "God, please, not on my birthday," before Ezra pulled me back. The shock sunk in as he called 911 and checked outside for any intruders who may have been responsible for stabbing Clive. I sat down in the nearest chair, my pulse thudding in my head.

I didn't know CPR or any first-aid techniques, and even if I did, Clive was bleeding out fast. Once again, the common regret of academics echoed throughout my thoughts: if I'd just gotten my doctorate in medicine, not Tolkien studies, perhaps I could save his life.

While Ezra called for help outside, I bent over Clive hesitantly. What could I do to help him, save his life? His face, grayish-purple, leered at me.

It was then that I saw one culprit of the thudding sound Ezra and I had heard, what made me suspect it must have been an unlucky bird at first.

Splayed out by Clive's body and splattered in blood, a copy of The Landlord's Game stared back up at me. The same that I'd haggled with and ultimately rejected Clive over today.

"Look at that." I laughed, out of reflex than true humor. "Live to regret it? Maybe I will. Or maybe . . ."

My vision went fuzzy around the edges until I wasn't sure which way was up or down. The next thud, I heard only with a dim awareness. My own body, collapsing against the ground.

I'd never fainted at the sight of blood before, but then, I'd also never seen so much of it.

Happy thirtieth birthday, indeed. I'd prefer the back pain everyone said I'd have by now. Nobody warned me about the possibility of being a murder witness.

Chapter 6

When I awoke, and the shock wore off, I was able to process that someone had wrapped a blanket around me and led me to a chair. Not an especially comfortable chair but, well . . . what comfort could anything offer after watching someone bleed out in front of my shop?

Ezra stood by me as the paramedics and ultimately police filtered in and out of the shop. He held my hand when they moved Clive away on a stretcher—a sheet over his body. My knowledge of such things only came from brief glimpses of crime shows I'd seen before switching the channel to something else. But even I knew a sheet over one's body was a grim sign.

"He'll be okay," I said, squeezing my eyes shut to forget the shade of purple his face had turned. "Won't he?"

Ezra started to answer, stopped, and then said in a gentler tone, "Your dad will be here soon, Ben. We can sit together until then."

I nodded and shivered, in part because of the cold let in by the open door. Our store heater worked surprisingly well (it had to, given the high altitude and how chilly things got), but it was not a miracle worker.

"I guess," I said slowly, "we'll have to take a rain check on that dinner date at your apartment?"

"The what?" Ezra looked at me with his head tilted; then he slapped his forehead. "Oh! Oh, jeez, Ben. In the shock of everything, I forgot."

"It's all right that you did. We'll probably have to stay for witness statements."

"For what it's worth . . . happy birthday." He sighed and shook his head. "No, that's tasteless. I'm sorry."

"Don't be. It's not as if you killed him."

One of the police officers on the scene approached me and Ezra shortly afterward. She looked, in a word, exhausted. She had dark circles under her eyes, probably from a career of unhappy cases like this one. Her uniform was somewhat rumpled, and I wondered if she had been off-duty when she got the call. She shook my hand, and though it didn't reach her eyes, her smile gave me some level of warmth.

"Ben Rosencrantz? I've been told you are the owner of Of Dice and Decks."

"I am," I said. "Well, my dad owns the shop, but I've been running it as of late."

"I'm Detective Louise Shelley," she said. "It's nice to meet you, Ben. I wish it were under better circumstances. How are you doing?"

"I'm okay as long as I don't think about it too hard," I said. "When I do, things get . . . overwhelming."

"I've been told you and your . . . companion," she said, eyeing Ezra and me as if unsure how to address us, "discovered Clive."

Detective Shelley and Ezra exchanged a look.

"To put it bluntly, he was pronounced dead at the scene."

"Horrible." I wrapped the blanket closer around my shoulders, pressing down nausea. "It's not murder . . . is it?"

As soon as the words left my mouth, Detective Shelley and I looked at each other. But instead of calling me an idiot (like I deserved, some might argue . . . people rarely just fall on knives), she said gently, "I don't think there's much you could have done. Were you close?"

I bristled at the way her question probed at something that felt darker. It was selfish, maybe, to think of it at the scene of a crime . . . but man, how I did not want to be accused of murder.

"No," I said. "Not at all. Apparently, he'd come into the shop from time to time, but I'd only ever met him once."

"When?"

"Today," I admitted. "He was trying to sell me a board game, actually, but I passed on it."

It was then that the memory came back to me: a copy of The Landlord's Game, right by Clive's body.

"I saw it!" I gasped.

Detective Shelley frowned. "I don't follow."

"The board game Clive wanted to sell me. It was right by his body—I think he must have dropped it after he knocked on our door."

"Hmm. Are you positive that you saw it tonight?"

"Yes. It's not a very common game, you see—copies in good condition can go for as much as one hundred grand. Sometimes more, depending on the quality."

Detective Shelley whistled. "I've never wondered what the amount is that would make a person kill another, but maybe it's that."

"Do you think . . . ?"

I let the question go unfinished.

"That someone came back for it?" said Detective Shelley. "We haven't seen any games next to Clive's body, no. It wasn't small enough that it could go unnoticed?"

I shook my head. "As large and wide as a Monopoly box."

"I see."

"I imagine you and Ezra weren't paying the most attention between discovering Clive and the time that the EMTs arrived, am I correct?"

Both of us shook our heads.

"I went to the streets to try and find help," said Ezra. "And Ben . . ."

"I was, uh, overwhelmed. I think I fainted. Did I?"

"You were conscious by the time I got back," said Ezra, "but on the floor. And not in the best emotional state, no."

"It's nothing to be embarrassed about," said Detective Shelley. "From what Ezra was telling me, Clive more or less died in your arms. Shock is expected."

"Oh, God. Can we, um? I mean, I know you'll probably need to get statements from us. But I think I need a moment to process . . ." I cleared my throat, feeling a little light-headed again. "Sorry. I just . . . never been one for gore. I couldn't even read *Crime and Punishment* with my freshmen. I'd get nightmares."

"Were you a teacher?"

"Oh, yes," I said wryly. "In another life, I was called Professor Rosencrantz."

"Not a Shakespeare professor, I hope?"

I wrinkled my nose. "Oh, no. No specifically. That would be a little too on the nose, wouldn't it?"

"You stay safe, Professor Rosencrantz," she said. "I will need to take statements from you and Ezra both, but it doesn't need to be tonight. Even if you didn't know Clive well, you may have information that can help my team if you're right about that missing board game. Your dad will be here soon?"

"He will," said Ezra before I could say anything. "Thank you, detective."

I wrung my hands as Detective Shelley walked away, quickly immersed in conversation with another officer. In life, Clive had been a brief nuisance to me; in death, he was shaping up to be the most likely thing to give me an ulcer.

"You don't think she suspects me, do you?" I asked.

"Because of the board game?" When I nodded, Ezra exhaled slowly. "I don't know if that's the biggest thing you need to worry about, Ben. You're a game shop owner. Of course you're going to know the details surrounding a rare game. Of course you're going to recognize it."

"She's right. The Landlord's Game is enough money for someone to kill over. If they were desperate. And I swear that I saw it."

"I believe you," said Ezra gently. "Maybe Clive was coming back to give you one last chance at it and just came across the wrong person on the way."

"If that's true, there must be some particularly geeky criminals here in Sugar House," I said bitterly. "Who else would know the value of a game like that? Probably not the average Salt Lake City citizen. It doesn't look good. You have to admit that."

"Sure. You know a lot about games. And you also fainted at the sight of blood," Ezra pointed out. "Not exactly murderous behavior."

I shuddered. But he was right.

"Give it a few days," said Ezra. "I don't think someone who would stab a man to death in the middle of a shopping neighborhood is the type of criminal cunning enough to avoid arrest. You don't happen to have a doorbell camera set up, do you?"

I shook my head. "We really don't stock things valuable enough to warrant it."

"Well, maybe someone nearby does. Nice Buns or Devil's Brewery. I promise—you and I have been through the worst of it. We were unlucky enough to witness what . . . what happened. Soon enough, though, they'll find whoever killed Clive."

"Unless we're next." Ezra shot me a look, and my shoulders sagged underneath the blanket. "Sorry."

Chapter 7

When the night was over, Dad's most pressing concern was Detective Shelley's words for him: close Of Dice and Decks for the weekend and reopen Monday. That, she said, would give forensics enough time to collect . . . I gagged . . . whatever evidence they needed to move the case forward.

This, he took hard for several reasons. One, he'd never closed the shop in its history unless he was so sick, he physically couldn't get himself there, or we were going on one of my few childhood vacations. As a single parent, he found that money wasn't exactly plentiful—every day closed meant his budget had to stretch further.

And despite the stress of running it, Of Dice and Decks was truly his. I hadn't been kidding when I said it was like a second child to him. One of his greatest fears when he got his diagnosis—late-onset muscular dystrophy, a condition that ran in our family—was that he'd ultimately have to sell or close down the store.

Detective Shelley's advice must have felt like an omen of things to come. Regardless, he closed the shop as he was told. Ezra and I gave the detective our contact information with plans to give our statements within the next few days. But by Sunday morning, it hadn't yet happened.

Dr. Petras invited me to breakfast at Nice Buns, to catch

up and (I assumed) to make sure we were doing all right after Clive's murder. Free breakfast I'd be hard-pressed to turn down regardless of who'd offered it, especially after such a troubling weekend. But I had missed her, and I welcomed the chance to spend time in their shop.

I left Dad's and my home while it was still dark out to get a quick jog in at the nearby Sugar House park. Despite the chill, a few ducks and geese hung around in the patches of grass uncovered by snow. Running helped to clear my mind, as did the chill November air, and clarity was what I desperately needed.

After I'd worked off a sufficient amount of nerves, I made my way to Yael and Dr. Petras's shop. Our street was in a part of the neighborhood that bore few differences from the nearby residential areas. While you could find the multistoried buildings typical of a city and the sprawling Westminster College campus in downtown Sugar House, most shops over here operated out of much smaller cottages—some as old as one hundred years.

Nice Buns was smaller in space than Of Dice and Decks (not an easy feat, as we weren't exactly spacious to begin with). There were only a few seated areas, coveted and usually claimed by regulars. But the customers didn't seem to mind, and the line to the register would stretch outside even in the cold weather. With the smell of warm bread, cinnamon, and icing as thick in the air as it was, I couldn't blame them.

Being family friends with the owner, of course, had its perks. By the time I got there, Dr. Petras was waiting in front with two cinnamon rolls larger than my head.

"I know this doesn't make up for a birthday like the one you had," she said before we dug in, "but I've found few situations in which baked goods can't at least offer a little comfort."

"They're always there for you," I agreed.

And indeed, I'd been surviving off comfort foods in the time since Clive's death. Takeout, mainly. Neither Dad nor I were proficient—or even competent—cooks. And if I set off the smoke alarm anytime soon, I felt so high-strung that I could easily give myself a heart attack.

"Have you heard anything new?"

"Not really. I'd guess the police are busy interviewing people. Maybe running DNA tests on the murder weapon. Is that how those things work?"

I'd heard very little from Detective Shelley on Saturday and had spent most of the day cuddled with my dog, Beans, under a large blanket and a (metaphysical) stack of comfort movies to watch.

Dr. Petras gave me a bracing smile. "I wouldn't know. Never had a brain for science, myself, let alone criminal science."

"No true crime, then?"

I'd asked her the question just as she took a large bite of the cinnamon roll. She held up her finger, then said, "That's more Yael's interest than mine."

"I'll have to talk to her before I go."

"You're not thinking of investigating yourself, are you?"

"Me? No."

The thought had flitted through my mind on the particularly sleepless parts of the past few nights. But ultimately, I sided with Ezra. It would probably be safer to let Detective Shelley conduct the investigation. And anyways, making conversation with my customers was already a challenge. I doubted I'd be any good at investigating suspects.

"I wanted to get a sense of what the investigation process looks like," I explained. "So I have an idea of how long it might be until the person responsible is found."

"I don't know if there's a standard length of time for something like this, Ben . . ." She trailed off. "But as I said, what do I know? Regardless, I can't imagine it's made the transition back to Utah any easier for you. A change of careers is one of the biggest stressors a person can experience behind divorce and death; did you know that? And, well . . ."

"I've experienced all three at once now." I rubbed the bridge of my nose. That certainly explained the headaches. "I'll admit, I miss teaching a lot. More than I thought I would've after my first year."

And I did. Public speaking had not come easy to me. I spent many nights in graduate school wondering if I had it in me to teach courses every day for the rest of my life.

But once I lost myself in a love of the subject, the anxiety tended to fade. Especially when I realized the students shared my interest in literature and discussing it with like-minded people.

After a while, I even started to enjoy it more than the research aspects of my work. I still thought about some of my students and hoped that, whoever had taken my position after I'd left, they never lost their love of reading.

"Do you think you'll ever return to it?" Dr. Petras asked lightly.

"If I could find somewhere that would have me, I would like to. Part-time, of course. Certainly Brigham Young University wouldn't hire me, but—"

"You wouldn't want a job there even if it came with tenure. They'd fire you the moment you started dating other men," said Dr. Petras drily. "Trust me. I did my time."

Dr. Petras had been expelled from the university long before I'd been born. BYU may have been one of the most prestigious universities in the state, but they showed little compassion for their queer students.

"I'll ask around," she continued. "You never know what openings there will be for spring, maybe even winter semester."

Dr. Petras was being generous with those ranges—by this late in fall, every college would have its schedule for the upcoming semester finalized—but I didn't correct her. With the holiday season approaching, Of Dice and Decks would keep Dad and me busy enough that I could wait until spring if I had to.

"Don't think I'm not sending out my CV. In between running the shop, I mean."

Ideally, I'd like to find somewhere that would allow me to teach one or two evening classes a semester. A local community college, perhaps. That way, I could supplement what income we earned from the shop with another means of earning money. Plus, such jobs sometimes included insurance, if you taught more than one and the institution in question was feeling merciful.

"And your dad's doing okay?"

"With the murder investigation or with his treatment?"

"Both," said Dr. Petras.

"The shop being closed troubles him, I can tell you that. But by Monday, I think he'll be in better spirits. He doesn't like being stuck at home with nothing to do." I groaned. "I don't know about that second part. He hardly talks to me about it."

"I can't imagine it's easy for either of you."

"It's not, but I wish he'd at least tell me what's on his mind. Whenever I ask, he changes the subject. But so far, the medication seems to be working well for him. He's been able to maintain his independence, and he has me here to do the heavy lifting for what he can't do."

"I don't pretend to be a mind reader," said Dr. Petras, "but I bet he's happy to have your help."

"It's probably good for both of us," I admitted. "Seattle was a wonderful place to live, when things were going well . . . but they hadn't been for a while."

Shane had always been the extroverted one between us— pulling me out of my shell and forcing me to interact with other human beings. Not always an easy task, but spending time outside of our home tended to make me feel better when I was low. Even if I was rarely the one to suggest it.

When he left, it became so much easier to stay inside weekend after weekend. There were lesson plans to prep, after all, and symposium papers to submit. And there were books, books I stacked up so high that I could block every-one else out if I wanted. Books could make for a cozy week-end, but they couldn't always numb the loneliness. They could wall you up inside yourself until you were all alone, if you let them.

"I'm sorry to hear about you and Shane," said Dr. Petras. "Truly. How are you coping?"

She said it in a way that indicated she had likely already asked Dad the same thing behind my back. I couldn't fault her for it, though. It was certainly easier to ask someone else if a person was hurting than to ask them to their face.

"It was amicable," I said. "Or at least that's the term our divorce attorney used. I suppose he'd know how to use that kind of jargon correctly, so why not."

Of course, it was easy enough for him to phrase it that way. He and Shane ran in similar circles—far away enough that no ethical issues presented themselves. But close enough that at least Shane remained comfortable through the process.

I, meanwhile, had felt as though my heart were going to give out from the pain. Though I'd tried not to let Shane in on that. Not because I thought he'd care, but because I didn't want to make things messier than they already were.

"I just don't understand what happened," I blurted out. "We loved each other. Or at least, I thought we did. Work kept us busy, sure, but I thought . . ."

"Oh, Ben." Dr. Petras grabbed my hand, and I resisted the urge to yank it back. "I know it must have been a shock. You two seemed happy together."

"I thought we were, once. But I guess if he was, he wouldn't have looked for happiness with someone else."

I said it quietly enough that no one in the shop looked our way. But with the words out in the open, I couldn't help but feel as if I were crumpling inward. Couldn't stop my shoulders from trembling, just a little.

I didn't like talking about my feelings, even with someone who had known me through my teenage angst phase like Dr. Petras had.

"I don't know what you're telling yourself, but it's not your fault," she said. Then, she added, "He didn't . . ."

"Cheat on me? No," I said, and it was true enough for what I wanted to share with Dr. Petras. He'd waited until we separated to make things official with his boyfriend. "He really wasn't a jerk. It would be easier to hate him if he was. He just . . . knows what he wants, and I guess that wasn't me anymore."

"Then he's just as foolish as BYU."

Despite myself, I laughed. It still hurt, thinking of Shane, but at least a little less. I had forgotten in Seattle that there were still people in the world who cared about me. Now that I was back home with Dad and Dr. Petras, I could hope that someday it wouldn't hurt at all.

"This is hardly a cinnamon roll conversation," I apologized. "I didn't mean to dampen the mood."

"You may not believe it, Ben, but I enjoy being around you." Dr. Petras smiled and, after finishing the last of her cinnamon roll, said, "Yael and I both. It's been a delight to watch you grow up, find your place in the world. If you don't trust yourself, then trust me: you'll be back on your feet soon enough. Give it a year or two, and you'll forget the divorce and the investigation even happened."

Before leaving, I stopped to ask Yael—who was preparing delivery orders in the back kitchen—how much she knew about true crime.

"Is this about the . . . you know."

She made a stabbing motion against her chest. I tried to push down my nausea, reminded of the sight of Clive's body in his last moments, and nodded.

"I like to listen to them while I work," she said. "In my headphones. Some of our employees get sick when I play them over the speakers."

"I . . . can't imagine why. Anyways," I said, "I was wondering if you happen to know how long it usually takes the police to find a killer. A week? Two?"

She raised her eyebrows.

"A month?" I said, my voice breaking slightly at the second word.

"Ben, do you know what a cold case is?"

"I'm familiar with the idea of them, but don't you think—"

She snorted and cut a length of ribbon to tie over the box of cinnamon rolls in front of her. "Then pray this incident with Clive doesn't become one."

Before driving back home, I picked up a sandwich for Dad from a nearby deli. He spent many a summer evening in their courtyards playing mini Nertz rounds with Kit, and so I hoped it would help him take his mind off the shop's temporary closure.

When I got home, my white-and-brindle Chihuahua, Beans, was curled up on a pillow near the coffee maker in the kitchen—still fragrant, which, as I scratched her behind the ears, I imagined is what drew her to it. When I'd adopted her years ago, the shelter didn't have much information on her except that her entire litter had been abandoned by someone cruel enough to do that to helpless puppies. She was so small that she fit in my cupped hands, and she shook constantly.

For the first few days, she hid underneath blankets and refused to emerge except for eating, and even then when I was in another room. Until after one insomnia-ridden night, I brewed myself a cup of coffee and saw a hesitant snout poking into the kitchen from the hallway.

The smell of coffee seemed to soothe her—almost a cruelty since, as she was a dog, she'd never be able to have some. But it had given her a name and made her morning routine predictable. If she could find somewhere soft in the vicinity of the coffee maker, she was content.

"I don't suppose you've seen Dad, have you?" I asked her, to which she tilted her head.

As if in response, a knock at the window interrupted my conversation with my dog. I looked up and, well, speak of the devil.

His wispy tufts of hair were mostly covered by his beanie, a blue knit one that he was rarely seen without, but the hairs that weren't seemed to stick up—as if they were just as irate as he was. He was wearing maybe the ugliest sweater I'd seen him wear in a while, a little number that would have done well at a Christmas party. That was a usual staple in Dad's closet. He liked to dress in a way that would make others think "oh, how tacky" or "someone should nominate this man for *Queer Eye*."

"A little late in the season for gardening, isn't it?" I said after meeting Dad on the back porch.

"Leaves." He gestured to a flat, orangish pile in the middle of the yard. "Beans is welcome to jump in them if she'd like."

I looked through the window at Beans, who lay napping below the coffee maker. Few things made her jump. Where other dogs got zoomies at the prospect of going on a walk, Beans got them when she returned home.

"That would take a . . . lot of convincing," I said. "Sure you don't want me to take care of the leaves?"

With Dad's new diagnosis, I tried to stay in conversation with him and his doctor about what was and was not all right for him to handle. But it seemed like for the most part, the answer was, "Leave it up to his comfort level and help where you can."

"If you wanted to do that, you should have come home earlier. I've just finished." He noticed the sandwich bag in my hand and stood up a little straighter. "Are those cold cuts? You shouldn't have."

At the mention of the words, Beans's snout poked out a little higher in the air. She could be eerie sometimes, when it came to food. As if she could understand us and our human problems, just for a moment, if the topic was delicious cured meats.

In response, I handed him the bag. Dad's love language was food. If he cared about you, he'd get you some food. And there was no better way to show him that you cared about him than picking him up a sandwich from his favorite deli. We were alike in that way.

I'd eaten one for myself in the parking lot, like some sort of wild bear that had developed a taste for pastrami and banana peppers.

"I'm gonna take Beans around the neighborhood," I said as Dad dug in, closing his eyes in contentment. "Let me know if you need anything, all right?"

"Thanks, Ben. I took her out earlier, but she refused to, well . . . you know. You'll have to see if you can get her to do it."

I rolled my eyes, grabbing Beans's leash off of the counter. Some times were clearer than others that Dad had limited experience with animals. "It's fine, I let her go in the backyard before you woke up. You've just got to wait it out until she does it. Remind her she doesn't have a choice—it's outside where she does it or nowhere."

As rousing as I'm sure our conversation about Beans's digestion habits was to Dad while he was trying to enjoy lunch, I wrestled Beans's harness, coat, and snow booties on and led her out the door with the leash.

"Be back in soon," I said. "Do you want me to pick anything else up?"

"Don't worry yourself." Dad scrutinized me. "Get some rest. You deserve it."

Beans knew perfectly well how to walk in her booties, but she tried to kick them off her back legs with each step as we made for the door. I'd hoped that in time, she'd accept that the booties were just part of going out in the cold weather. But despite the fact that they protected her from frostbite and had cost me a baffling forty dollars plus shipping, her opposition to them got stronger the more often she wore them.

"Hey," I said to her in a low voice, as if she were a misbehaving toddler that the neighbors might judge me for. "Knock it off, all right? Those are good for you. Keep your paws warm."

She looked up at me with large, baleful eyes. She was as keen as a person when food was involved, but—or at least it seemed to me—purposefully refused to understand when it came to why she had to go on a walk or wear little shoes. If it were up to her, she'd rarely leave her blankets and become indistinguishable from a sentient throw pillow.

To be fair, the little shoes were ridiculous. But I wasn't about to argue with a dog.

"Believe you me, I'd rather be inside where it's warm." I patted my chest to emphasize myself. "But I do this for you. Not my own joy. You."

She studied me, and for a second, I thought she understood. Her brows knit, as if in the most complex thought of her life. Perhaps she was considering the existential implications of not only her snow booties but the fact that she was a tiny dog in a cold, sometimes unforgiving world.

Then she lifted her leg to go pee, and I remembered that this was a dog I was trying to reason with and that maybe I should reconsider my dog-rearing tactics.

When she was done, I nudged her along. After a few minutes, we got into a rhythm. Or as close as one could get into a rhythm while walking a dog as stubborn as Beans. She stopped trying to tug off her shoes, and I almost felt like I was walking a reasonable dog.

After I got back home, there was what appeared to be a package waiting on the doorstep.

No, not a package, I realized as I got closer. A backpack.

It wasn't a particularly unusual one. It just wasn't mine. It was blue, a little scuffed. And it smelled even from this distance of body odor.

I had seen this backpack before. If I wasn't mistaken, it had last been worn by Clive.

"Great," I said, bending down to get a closer look. "If there's another dead body in this, that's it. I am going to move back to Seattle. If they don't lock me up first, that is."

I opened the backpack, and bills spilled out—not the worst of things that could have spilled out, I supposed, but given the context, I gasped. It was stuffed to the brim with crisp twenty- and hundred-dollar bills. I took a step back, as if I had just unboxed a snake.

"Oh, this is bad," I muttered. "This is very bad."

Or maybe it wasn't bad? I mean, I didn't know who it was from. Whether you could just take money that showed up at your house was also beyond my legal understanding. I knew that if you found probably a one-dollar bill on the ground, you could keep that. But what about ten thousand dollars? Maybe more? I'd never been good at counting or anything to do with math, so I was stumped on two levels.

I called Detective Shelley, eyeing the stuffed backpack and finally understanding the myth of Tantalus. Broke or not, I figured that I kind of had to inform her about strange happenings.

She picked up on the first ring, practically a half-ring. I was so impressed at her quick reflexes that I nearly stayed silent. "Sorry to bother you!"

"Professor Rosencrantz?"

"You don't have to call me that," I said. "You're not a student."

"What would you like me to call you? Mr. Rosencrantz?"

"Just Ben would be perfect."

"Then, Ben, you should know that you never have to apologize for calling me. What's going on?"

"I think I found something that could be related to the case."

"That quickly?"

"Well, I don't know for sure, but I can't shake the feeling . . ." I rubbed the back of my neck. "It's a backpack."

"A backpack," she said. "Where did you find it?"

"On my doorstep. I don't know how long it's been there, but I can ask my dad if he saw anything. It can't have been long."

"You never know what's inside a strange backpack. They're as ominous on a doorstep as they are in an airport. I'd ask you to see what's inside, but I'd like to inspect it first. Do you have any idea of what it might be?"

Now that she phrased it like that . . . perhaps I shouldn't have touched a stray backpack without knowing who it belonged to or what was in it. She made it seem so obvious.

"I don't know," I said. "Backpacks don't usually show up on my porch, is all. Especially not ones stuffed with money."

"So you've opened it." She muttered what sounded like a swear word under her breath, then said, "When we say 'stuffed' . . ."

"I've never been good with money—I failed algebra twice." I laughed, more out of nerves than anything. "But it's more than I've seen in one place, for what it's worth."

"I'll come down to pick it up shortly."

Beans shivered and pawed at the door. "Do I have to stay outside until they take it?"

"Do you have anywhere else to be?" she probed. "I was under the assumption your shop was closed."

"It is," I reassured her. "But my dog . . . I was just taking her on a walk."

"Put the dog inside, but please wait outside if you can. With The Landlord's Game disappearing right when you weren't looking at it, I'd prefer to avoid any similar situations."

Was I just paranoid, or did I note suspicion in Detective Shelley's voice? I supposed if I were her, I'd see the backpack full of money and the disappearing game as troubling.

"I know how this looks," I said, clinging to the phone as if it were my one chance to not get booked in jail today. "But—"

"I'm not going to arrest you, if that's what you're worried about," she said. "You're a suspect, of course. As is your father. As is every witness and several others who weren't there. But I don't make arrests unless I have a reason to do so, I can promise you that."

I closed my eyes and took a few seconds to respond so I wouldn't sound too emotional over the phone. "Thank goodness for that. It feels weird to just have a backpack full of money lying around. You sure I shouldn't put it inside?"

"Yes," she said firmly. "Please don't move it or touch it at all. If you already have, that's okay, but I'd like as little tampering as possible."

"All right," I said. "Will you be here soon?"

"Within the hour."

As promised, Detective Shelley and a few other police officers arrived just in time for me to explain what was going on to Dad, who swore he saw nobody deliver the backpack, as he was too busy experiencing sandwich bliss in the kitchen.

They removed the backpack from the porch steps without thankfully too much commotion.

"And you're certain neither of you saw who dropped the bag off?" said Detective Shelley to Dad and me.

I looked at Dad, who shook his head. I resisted the urge to shudder. It gave me the creeps to think of someone with possibly sinister intentions leaving something by our house without either of us noticing.

"I didn't, either," I said. "It was on the doorstep by the time I came home."

"From where?"

"Walking Beans. She can be . . . cumbersome to walk. She doesn't like the snow."

"I wouldn't if the snow were taller than me, too."

"Yes, well. Don't tell her that. She'll feel vindicated in how difficult she makes it. I didn't see anyone near our house when I left or returned, though. I don't suppose you've recovered the copy of The Landlord's Game . . . ?"

"We have not," said Detective Shelley. "But perhaps this is an indication it's been sold—maybe not by Clive, but by someone."

"Not me," I said. "If I wanted the game that badly, I would have just bought it from Clive."

Detective Shelley scrutinized me. "That would certainly be the easier route."

Unless someone didn't want to pay. Unless someone was desperate. Though unspoken, the thoughts must have been as loud in her mind as they were in mine.

"I don't know what we did to deserve this," said Dad.

"It may not be a question of deserving but of convenience. You and your son own a board game shop. Perhaps Clive had arranged to meet someone there."

"We were closed," said Dad. "And if Clive had enough sense to get himself there, he would know that."

"I know," said Detective Shelley, sharper than I'd heard her talk before. "That's the part I'm trying to work out."

She took the opportunity to get Dad's and my statements in the living room. Despite my lingering carpal tunnel from my grading days, I gave her as many details as I could—

Clive's insistence on underselling the game, the weird phone call I'd heard near our shop, and the approximate time Ezra and I had heard him knock on the door before collapsing at my feet.

I could feel a marked shift in Detective Shelley's interactions with me after the matter of the backpack. And I could hardly blame her. A valuable board game goes missing, with a man dead and a large backpack of cash found on a board game shop owner's doorstep? It had the makings of an open-and-shut case if the right evidence arose.

As we talked, the officers with her conducted a search of our house—with our permission. "Just in case," she said, "the person who left the money broke in without you knowing. They may have left something to reveal their identity."

If you asked me, however, I'd assume she was looking for Clive's game—or something else that would point to its sale.

Though I'd describe myself as agnostic at best, I prayed that Clive's murder would not go the way of a cold case. Because if the best evidence Detective Shelley had was circumstances that—even coincidentally—pointed to me, then how much would it take for her to arrest me?

Chapter 8

After the detective and her team left, I sat down on the couch with Beans on my lap, petting her absently.

She closed her eyes halfway and radiated contentedness. Not for the first time, I wished my life were as simple as hers.

"Ben?"

I jolted. Dad frowned at me from the hallway.

"Didn't mean to scare you. I called your name a few times."

"Sorry," I said. "I think my brain is just trying to process what happened."

"It's not your fault."

I shook my head. "I know. But it doesn't really matter, does it? All that matters is whether the detective thinks it's my fault."

"They won't. They'll figure out whoever actually did it."

"How?"

Dad paused. If there had been any straws in the room, he'd be grasping at them.

"DNA . . . fingerprinting . . . dang it, I don't know. But they have science."

"Maybe. But the copy of The Landlord's Game certainly has my fingerprints on it now. What if the person who killed Clive wore gloves?"

Dad swore under his breath. "Gloves. I didn't even think about that. You don't think they'd be that cunning, do you?"

"Who? The person who murdered Clive? I don't think they'd care about what is or isn't fair game. And gloves are hardly high-tech."

Our conversation, which was mainly whispered despite the fact that Beans was the only person in the room, was interrupted by a knock at the door.

I jumped again.

"Ben, really, you need to calm down." Dad stood up. "I'll get the door."

I listened to his footsteps as he went down the hallway, a heaviness mounting in my chest. Was it the detective, here to arrest me for a crime I never committed?

"It's for you," Dad called.

I set Beans down on the couch and petted her a few times. If this was the last time I ever saw her, I wanted her to remember me like . . . this? Clammy hands, one more round of bad news away from absolute broken sobbing?

She closed her eyes and gave a snort. She was snoring.

She'd fallen asleep.

I hurried down the hall to the front door. "Detective, I—"

I stopped mid-sentence at the two people staring back expectantly at me. Dad at the door and, on the porch with a bouquet of orange and blue flowers in his hand, Ezra.

"Did they—"

"Take my statement, yes," said Ezra. "They seemed in a rush, too. Did something new happen?"

"We found a backpack full of hundred-dollar bills on the porch. I think someone's either trying to frame me for Clive's murder or pay me off." I paused. "And I don't know which would be worse."

Ezra whistled. "That's worse than I thought. A more gung-ho officer might have arrested you for less."

"But you don't think so?"

Ezra rolled his eyes. "Do you want me to be honest?"

"Of course."

"I don't think you have it in you. I think you'd sooner apologize for running into a tree than kill a spider, let alone a person."

"It's less messy if you put them in a cup and let them out. And humane. Everyone knows that."

Ezra grinned. "Exactly my point. I know this is a bad time, before you ask, but I have an idea."

"And the flowers?" said Dad.

Ezra looked down at them, eyebrows raised, as if he himself had forgotten that he'd brought them. "I panicked."

After placing the flowers in a vase in the kitchen, Dad and I sat Ezra down in the living room and shakily explained to him how my questioning with Detective Shelley had gone. Every so often, he interrupted with a question, but for the most part, he just listened.

"It was similar for me," he said, "except that the conversation dropped off around when I said I didn't know Clive. It sounds like he was a customer of yours?"

"Barely," said Dad. "We don't deal in collectibles. Too many strange people."

"Apparently so," said Ezra. "What kind of person kills someone else for a Monopoly prototype?"

"It's more than a prototype," said Dad. "It's a historical artifact. Monopoly's the most popular board game there is, and this is the game it stole everything from."

"I suppose we don't know for sure that's why he was killed . . ." I trailed off. "But I can't shake the timing of it all. Either way, I'm probably a suspect. I was one of the last people to talk to him."

"Right," said Ezra. "And that's where my idea comes in."

"Unless you can un-murder Clive," said Dad, "I don't know what good ideas will do."

"Well, I can't do that, but maybe we can try the next best thing." Ezra hunched over, his hands raised as he explained. "Last night after I got home, I was playing an old favorite. A point-and-click detective game from the nineties."

"Relaxing."

"It was. There was this part where the main character is cornered by the big bad guy. And he says, 'Sometimes, the only way out of danger is through it.'"

"What does he do then?" I asked.

"He kicks the big bad guy in the jaw. It's a very violent video game."

I glanced out the window. It would have been a beautiful day if not for the murder looming over our heads.

"Ezra, I don't see what this has to do with anything."

"I thought I made myself obvious. We can't just sit around and hope you don't get charged. We need to find the person who really did this, and we need to make them confess."

"Even if we could do that," I said, "how would we make a likely armed and definitely unhinged person turn themselves in?"

Ezra scratched his chin. "Well, usually in the games, they start monologuing. You just need to record that and turn it in to the police."

Despite myself, I smiled. It was a small smile, but I couldn't help myself around him sometimes.

"I don't know that I'd be good at solving murders," I said. "I can barely manage a regular conversation with strangers. The anxiety gets the best of me most times, and that would be a hindrance."

"Fair enough. Then I guess we'll have to rely on our senses."

"We?"

Ezra blinked. "Of course. You didn't think I'd just abandon you?"

"Well . . ."

"Ben, really. Would you abandon me?"

I shook my head vehemently. "Of course not. But I know you have your shop to tend to. You can't just drop your life because of my misfortune."

Ezra waved me off. "And I won't have to. We can do it in our free time."

"Suppose I said yes," I said slowly. "Where would we start?"

"Usually, the detective starts interviewing people." Ezra rested his head on his hands. "People who might have seen the murder. Or people who might have committed it."

"Dad."

Ezra's eyes went wide as he looked between me and my father. "I highly doubt your dad falls into either of those categories."

"No, I mean he'd probably know who best to talk to. I'm ten years removed from the gaming scene here. He's sold items to them every day for decades. Right?"

Uncomfortable with both Ezra's and my eyes on him, Dad shrugged stiffly. "I may have some ideas, yes."

"I don't know," I said. "Wouldn't that just make things worse?"

"How so?"

"It could look suspicious if I start talking around town, asking after Clive."

"So long as you don't go murdering other people, I don't see what the problem with that would be."

"I didn't even murder one!" I cried.

Ezra must have noticed how shaken up I was about the whole thing, because he squeezed my arm.

"I know you didn't," he said. "I didn't meant to imply anything. I just thought that maybe if you exerted some control over the situation, you'd feel better."

"I've never been in any situation like this," I said. "I just don't know what would help, but I'm afraid of what could hurt my case."

"You said that you're worried that you're being framed, right?" said Ezra.

"Yes," I said slowly. "Why else would the backpack be on my doorstep, right?"

"Maybe I have a sleepwalking problem that we don't know about," said Dad. "A very murderous one."

"If there is someone trying to frame you," said Ezra, "then it stands to reason that someone could be putting in all this work against you. So if you don't do something about it, what if you fall right into their trap?"

I struggled to speak for a few moments, and when I did, it was weak. "But I don't *want* to do that. All I wanted was to sell games, drink my London Fog, and try not to think about my divorce. This is all so much to deal with."

"You're not dealing with it alone, Ben," said Dad firmly. "You'll always have me."

"And me, too," said Ezra. "Like I said, you've been a stellar friend to me. Friends don't let friends get framed for crimes they didn't commit."

I met eyes with Beans, hoping that she would give me some form of puppy-dog wisdom. It might have been a coincidence, but she winked.

"I'll think about it," I said. "But even if we did start asking around, I wouldn't know where to start."

"That's an easy one," said Dad. "We're not the only game shop in Salt Lake City. I bet Clive was selling to other places, too."

"Sure," I said, "but that would mean going to . . ."

We exchanged a meaningful look.

"Give me some time," I said. "Maybe an hour or two. I don't think your idea is a bad one. I just want to make sure there's nothing I'm not considering."

"Of course," said Ezra. "You have my number, right? Call me if you need anything else. I've got a few arrangements to deliver, but after that, all I've got going on is babysitting my sister's kids. If there's an emergency, I can try and help how I can."

After he left, I figured the best thing for thinking things through would be sleep. Maybe it would awaken something in my subconscious mind, help me figure out who could possibly have wanted both me and Clive in hot water. It's not like, besides board games, we had all that much in common.

Unfortunately, the only sleep I got was troubled and sweaty. I had not even considered the toll that today would take on me in terms of nightmares.

Chapter 9

❧

"B-eight."

"Dang it. Hit."

I winced at my heavily destroyed plastic ship fleet and called out a number of my own. Beans sniffed at the board and looked up at me with her beady little eyes, as if asking permission to eat at least one of the pieces.

I shook my head at her and gently pushed her snout away from the board.

Dad smirked. "Miss. A-nine."

I took a few moments to respond, then rubbed my temples. "You . . . you sunk my ship. Again."

"Of course I did. Was that the last one?"

He took my silence as confirmation (which it was) and pumped the air with his fist. Dad was never a sore loser, mostly because he rarely lost, but he definitely tried to make others one sometimes.

Seeing a dead body was definitely a setback, and closing the shop for a few days was another—to put it lightly—but I wasn't going to let it get in the way of Dad's and my game night. You'd think after a few decades of selling the things, he would be bored (no pun intended) of them and refuse to play when he was out of the shop. Or at least get all snobby about the board games he chose to play.

But he'd started the shop because he genuinely loved them—all of them, not just the ones non-enthusiasts had never heard of. In a way, gaming was his love language.

I tried to laugh along with him, but try as I might, my heart wasn't in it. All I could manage was a weak smile while absently patting Beans on the back. Beans, at least, closed her eyes in contentment.

He caught sight of me and frowned as I started putting the game pieces back in the box. "It's Clive, isn't it?"

"I didn't even know the guy, Dad. I saw him once. And now, I'm worried that everyone'll be looking at me as if they're wondering who I'll go after next."

"That's not true. And I'll vouch for you if anyone does." He pointed at a piece. "That one's in the wrong spot."

"Did you see me between the hours of the last time anyone saw Clive living—which very well might have been me—and when he turned up dead?" When Dad didn't respond, I sighed and picked up the box. "I'm just worried. If I can't work, the shop will have to close. And we can't afford that."

"It won't. We have Sophie. She could manage it for a bit." He tried to sound confident, but I could hear the doubt in his voice. "It won't help you or me to keep brooding over it. Action—action is helpful. What can we do to clear you? That's what we should be thinking about."

He picked up the board game out of my hands and headed for the shelf. "And I can take that back. Don't trouble yourself; you're a guest here."

His muscular degeneration hadn't progressed to the point where the box was too heavy for him—especially not such a light board game—but I still had to bite my tongue when I watched him.

I also didn't remind him that technically, I lived here too now. Indefinitely. Partially because I didn't want to make him feel bad, but also, when I really thought about it, it made me feel like a bit of a failure that I was sleeping in the same room that I had as a teenager again.

"I've been thinking about it. What I could do to at least clear myself, keep the shop open." I glanced over at him to gauge his expression. "The only thing I can really think of is to figure out who did it, or at least point the police in the right direction."

To my surprise, Dad didn't. Seem surprised, I mean.

"Not a bad idea. You could at least see if other people know what's going on. Maybe somebody knows something that would at least give the police a better suspect."

"I've been wanting to ask you that, actually. You know Sugar House much better than me. All my information is twenty years outdated."

Dad raised his bushy eyebrows, his expression bemused. "You want me to give you a few names?"

"If you'd like."

"Of what? People who I think might have killed Clive?"

"Not necessarily," I said lightly, ignoring the chill that came down my spine as I considered what it would be like talking to potential murderers. "People who might have information would help."

He sat down on his armchair with a grunt and motioned me over. "Get me a pen and some paper. I'll give you some places to start, but only if you don't tell them I did. Don't want anyone to think I'm nosy."

I must have watched Dad scribble down in his notebook for a minute or so before he handed it back to me. When he did, he seemed rather proud of himself.

"This isn't an exhaustive list," he clarified. "Clive was . . . someone that more people disliked than liked. I wouldn't say *hated*, but he knew how to irritate."

"Isn't it bad luck to speak ill of a dead man?" I said, more to myself, as I looked through his list.

"Maybe. So it's a good thing I don't believe in luck."

The list had three names, though only one of them was an actual person:

- Jamie (Sugar House Computer Repair)
- Geek Chic (you know who)
- Salty Con

Of those, I only recognized one. Geek Chic, the *other* gaming store in Salt Lake City. If you were to say that there couldn't have been room for two shops in such a small area, you'd be right. We were constantly trying to run each other off and be the shop who survived. We had the advantage of being the older shop, and Geek Chic had the mall location going for it.

I also, unfortunately, knew the owner better than I would prefer.

"From what I understand, Clive built computers when he wasn't trying to sell people junk. Jamie's the one who runs the shop." He rubbed the bristles on his chin. "She's a good person, though I question her judgment in employing Clive."

I nodded. I'd spent much of my youth trying to figure out how computers worked—back when they were a lot less user-friendly than they are now—so I hoped I could use that to at least seem knowledgeable and not too "tell-me-where-you-buried-the-body."

"Salty Con—that's the new gaming convention, right?"

Utah was easily one of the geekiest states in the country, and it was honestly a surprise such a convention hadn't existed before now. Salty Con had begun several years ago, after I'd begun teaching in Seattle. I'd kept meaning to visit it, but my time off had never aligned.

I only wished that I could have visited it under better circumstances.

"It is. There's usually at least one or two vendors who deal in board game collections. If you ask around, you may be able to find someone who knew Clive better than we did."

"I'll take it. You're sure about Geek Chic?"

Dad nodded. "I don't like the idea of you going there any more than you do. But odds are, we weren't the only person Clive was selling collectibles to. Maybe he went there first that day. Maybe he told them more."

"I'll go. Or I'll get Ezra to go."

"There it is with Ezra again." Dad suddenly looked more somber. "He certainly seemed worried about you today. If there is really something going on between you . . . I know it took some time for me to understand. But I don't want you to feel like you can't talk with me about him. Or Shane, for that matter. I know that must have hurt."

Awkwardly as it came out of his mouth, I knew that he never would have said that when I was growing up. He'd come a long way. And though it took him until I was almost thirty to actively ask about my love life—and I didn't know that I wanted him doing that to begin with—it touched me, in a strange sort of way.

"There really isn't." I cleared my throat and folded the paper into quarters, feeling a little more fidgety than usual. "But thanks. For the list. And for saying that."

He winced. "Come on, you don't have to thank me. I'm old, but I'm still your dad."

I tried not to think about the fact that he was growing old. Or anything to do with mortality, really.

"Right. Sorry." I stood up, brushing my pants, and headed for the door. "This is a great starting point. I'm going to call—"

"Ezra," Dad finished for me.

"Well . . . yes," I said stiffly. "Ezra. But please tell me if you need anything else. You took your evening meds?"

"Does it look like I took my meds?"

"I don't think that's associated with a particular expression, so I don't know how to answer that."

"Oh? It's this one." He stared me down, deadpan. "'Night, Ben."

Ezra didn't pick up at first, which led me to worry if all the investigation talk had scared him off. If the situation were reversed, I'd have been more than a little hesitant. But when he called me back—while I was brushing my teeth, which led to a frantic and somewhat messy scene—he sounded out of breath.

"Sorry—sorry for missing your call, I just—"

"Is this a bad time?"

"No, no, no, no," he brushed me off. "I'm just watching my nieces tonight. They're two years old, but they have the energy of fully grown rabbits. And the intensity of a rabid dog."

"I'm told that's why they call it the terrible twos," I mused, which got a snort from Ezra. "I don't want to distract you."

"Don't worry. They're asleep. For now, at least."

"They're your sister's?"

"Yes, indeed. She's a little paranoid when it comes to babysitting. I'm the only one that she trusts."

"I see." I hesitated; then I said the riskiest thing I had ever leaped to in terms of invitations. "If you like . . . I mean, if it would be less distracting than a phone conversation . . ."

"You want to discuss this in person?"

Ezra sounded amused. I was glad someone could take humor in my nervousness.

The house was so picturesque middle-class suburbia that it even had a LIVE, LAUGH, LOVE sign hanging over the doorway. It smelled of vanilla and brown sugar, so pleasant that it almost made my heart hurt considering all of the general unpleasantness in my life lately.

I found Ezra in the kitchen, wearing a KISS THE COOK apron that hung well over his wiry frame and scrubbing the stove. I cleared my throat and he jolted, then half-smiled as he gestured at the scrubbie in his hand.

"You would be surprised how far and often toddlers fling macaroni and cheese."

"You poor, tired man."

"Don't 'poor Ezra' me." He pulled me a chair from the dining room table and sat down across from me on his own. "I'm much more worried about you."

"You know," I said, exhaling in a way that somehow made me feel heavier. "Me, too. I keep worrying that either the person who killed Clive will come after me next or they'll somehow frame me for the crime."

"Paranoid. But fair."

"My dad put together a list." I handed it to Ezra. "People who may know something. Or at least, people my dad thinks could know something."

"See what I mean? Martin is clever. I'd trust him." Ezra pored over it while hunched over the table. "So you want to investigate, then?"

"Yes. No. Well—I don't want to, but I think you're right. It's better than just sitting around and hoping I don't get framed for murder." I added, "And if you can do some of the talking for me, we may actually get somewhere."

"I would be honored. Any video game shops on the list?"

"No, why? Is there someone you might know?"

"Oh, no, nothing like that. I've been meaning to get a certain video game and, you know . . . if we happen to be in the neighborhood . . ."

I closed my eyes. "I think the computer repair shop where Clive used to work is next to a GameStop."

"Silver linings to everything." Ezra folded up the paper and handed it back to me. "We could start there, unless you could think of anywhere better. Maybe tomorrow?"

"I can't tell if you're more eager to help me or get your game."

"I contain multitudes."

We were interrupted by a hissing sound; the only comparison which I could even think of would be a demonic, sentient water faucet. I saw . . . something akin to a tangled gray mop move out of the corner of my eye. And then, it jumped on me.

I screamed as Ezra grinned and patted his lap. "Grandpa! Come here, boy!"

Despite my thoughts mostly being incoherent, my mind finally connected what the evil ball of yarn really was. It was a cat. The angriest, buggiest-eyed cat I had ever seen. Its fur puffed out around it like those lizards that have ruffs around them. It looked as if it would like nothing better than to kill me, personally.

"Oh right, you haven't met Grandpa yet," said Ezra, patting the thing that was mostly shaped like a cat. "You're not allergic, are you? The kids love him."

Grandpa looked like he would sooner eat children than tolerate being around them. But then, I'd never been raised around cats.

"No, not allergic," I said, keeping my gaze at Grandpa's level in case he tried to attack. "He's not allergic to professors, is he?"

"What?"

A little voice in my head reminded me that insulting Ezra's cat, unhinged as it appeared to be, would probably not endear me to him. Still breathing deeply, I said, "Never mind. Nice to meet . . . Grandpa."

"If Grandpa could talk, I'm sure he would say the same." Ezra checked his phone, the motion of which made Grandpa bristle. He most certainly did not look as if he wanted to say hello. "Hmm, quarter to eleven . . . if it were my place, I'd let you crash on the couch."

I waved my hand. "Don't worry about it. Now that I've been at my dad's for a month, I don't think he knows how to sleep alone."

Ezra walked me to the door and patted my shoulder. "You're good to him, you know. Better than you think. Monday, let's say during your lunch break? Of Dice and Decks will be open by then, right?"

"Yes," I said, eyes still on Grandpa—whose cruel head was staring around the corner, glinting at me. "Sorry to disrupt your babysitting. Being around you just makes me feel like I'm getting somewhere."

"People usually said the opposite of me in group projects," said Ezra, "so I appreciate it. 'Night, Ben."

"Goodnight, Ezra."

Chapter 10

We were able to reopen Monday, as Detective Shelley had re-assured us. Besides the odd question from customers about whether a body had really been found on our doorstep, business continued without a noticeable change in the number of customers willing to visit our shop. Ezra and I made plans to conduct our first investigation at Geek Chic that afternoon, after he finished delivering his orders for the day and could take a late lunch break.

After Dad arrived to start his shift at two, I waited for Ezra to arrive on the park bench outside our front walkway. I drummed my fingers on the arm rest.

I didn't want to go to Geek Chic on my own for a variety of reasons. For one, they were our greatest competitor in Salt Lake County—a contest that they, for the most part, were winning. And the owner brought up memories for me that I'd rather not revisit.

"Ben? What are you doing out here?"

I turned behind me to see Leon walking down the path, his hand tightly gripping his messenger bag.

"Ezra's meeting me here. We're going to go ask around Geek Chic about Clive, see if they know why he was acting so suspicious before . . ."

"Before he died?"

"Well. Yes. Before that." I sighed. "Ezra thinks if I can give the police any helpful evidence that points to me not killing Clive, it will help my case. And I have the afternoon off, anyways."

Leon's brow furrowed. "The police think you did it?"

I nodded. "I found one of his rare games on the shop's doorstep, but it disappeared before the police could collect it for evidence."

"I see." Leon's mouth made a flat line.

"I know what it sounds like, yes, and I'm sure the police do, too. Who knows? Maybe they think Ezra's my accomplice, and I'm making this even worse."

"That's absurd. I mean, look at you."

Leon gestured wildly at me, up and down. This reminded me all too much of Ezra's assertion that I'd be more likely to run into a tree than be capable of crimes. Or something.

I narrowed my eyes. "I don't quite see your point, Leon."

"I don't think you could even push someone over if you wanted to. Like, gun to your head."

"Love the vote of confidence."

"I'm serious. If I were the police, I'd look somewhere else. Someone who actually had a motive to kill Clive."

I cocked my head to the side. "Oh, yeah? Like who?"

Leon's shoulders hunched. He looked around, as if worried that any one of these small business owners was lurking behind a bush with a recording device and a sharp knife for making sure he never spoke again.

"Like his brother," Leon whispered.

"Who's—oh, I see. Clive has a brother?"

"*Had* a brother. You wouldn't have known him. He's not a collector like Clive. Also, he hated his guts."

"Really." I turned a little closer to Leon. "I don't want to put you on the spot, but do you know him well? Maybe you could give me his phone number."

Leon shook his head. "Not well, no. You going to Clive's funeral on Saturday?"

Clive's funeral? I guess it had crossed my mind that he would have one. But somehow it seemed inappropriate that I, a potential suspect with only minimal previous contact with the man, would go pay my respects.

"I wasn't planning on it," I said. "Do you think I should?"

Leon shrugged. "I know his brother will probably be there. And if you're really going to throw yourself out there and pretend to be a gumshoe, then I'm rooting for you."

"Thank you. I'll think about it." I glanced down at his messenger bag. "Done with work for the day?"

He smiled grimly. "With the passion project, yes. The well's run a little dry with freelance work. I've got a cousin who does electrician work, though. He's running me on a few errands for him."

"Is that legal to do if you're not certified?" When all Leon could give me was an ambivalent shrug, I dropped it. "You know what? It's not my business. Sorry to hear that, Leon. Best of luck."

After bidding him goodbye, I cursed myself for forgetting to ask him what Clive's brother's name even was. Though if there was only one of them, and I did decide to attend the funeral, perhaps I'd be able to figure it out by context.

But even if I did come across this supposedly suspicious brother, then what? I hadn't yet planned for what I'd do if I got my own suspects. Follow them around? Ask them pointed questions until they burst into guilty shrieks like an Edgar Allan Poe character?

No, thank you. That sounded uncomfortable for everyone involved.

When Ezra arrived, he sat down next to me on the bench, crossed his legs, and frowned. "You all right?"

"Yeah, I'm . . . do you think I should go to Clive's funeral?"

Ezra scrutinized me. "To investigate or to alleviate your conscience?"

"Both? No, the former. I don't know." I put my head in my hands. "Leon says Clive's brother is sketchy, or at least that they didn't get along. Maybe I could observe him at the funeral service."

"How would Leon know that?"

"Clive taught the after-school chess club at his high school, from what I understand."

"That would do it."

"It's not just that," I said. "Somehow, I can't help but feel that I'm connected to this. Obviously, I didn't kill him, but I feel . . . responsible isn't the right word. But I keep worrying that maybe if I'd just known the right first aid—"

"I don't think CPR or the Heimlich maneuver would have stopped him from bleeding out," Ezra said. "You're not at all responsible. You know that, right?"

"I've tried so hard to shake the feeling, but I can't. But I think maybe if I see the service and it's nicely attended, that his family at least gets some solace out of it, it will ease my guilt."

"Ben—" He stopped when he saw my face. "Have you been eating?"

"Well enough."

"Eat something before we go to Geek Chic. You look so shaken." He uncrossed his legs. "If you think it will give you solace, I say attend the funeral."

"It wouldn't be ghoulish?"

"No. Just because you didn't know him well doesn't mean you're not going through some sort of grief." He made a face. "Death is funny like that."

"Well, I wish it would stop being funny with our lives."

Geek Chic was one of those stores where I avoided the whole Sugar House Commons, it was located in downtown, just because looking at it made me so angry. It wasn't that it was painted a bad color (their aesthetic was "on point," as the kids say . . . or said within the span of fiveish years, who knew anymore) or that they sold crappy items (they generally had a good selection).

It's that they were newer, trendier, and better at marketing than Of Dice and Decks. They stole a good amount of our customers, apparently even the scummy ones like Clive. It didn't matter if they were a nice gaming shop or not. Ever since the Internet came about, running a board game shop has been a cutthroat business. You can't help but hate your competitors.

And besides that, the owner—a Mr. Craig Bird—had once been my youth group leader. Even though neither Dad nor I had ever joined the Mormon church, I attended the neighborhood youth activities group often as a teenager in an attempt to fit in and make friends. It hadn't worked and, while Craig had been nice enough to me, we remained little more than acquaintances. In part because he ran a store with the potential to put Dad's out of business.

"If you behave," said Ezra in a low murmur as we strode through the Commons, "I'll buy you a pretzel after."

I rolled my eyes. "You really know how to take a guy right back to junior high."

"In that case, I apologize. Anyways, this doesn't seem like the kind of mall that sells pretzels. It's a little too fancy."

He was right. The Sugar House Commons was an outdoor mall, and it was the sort that was trendy enough to survive where other malls died out. Between every shop was a restaurant or two, anchoring the shopping center's sales. There were several pubs, sure, but mall pretzels? I would be astonished to find one.

"Little farther . . . and there." I stopped and stuffed my hands in my pockets. "There it is. Our arch nemesis."

The Geek Chic sign—complete with a little horn-rimmed

glasses logo at the end—flashed with neon lights around the edges. Pop punk bounced out of the building like an over-caffeinated teenager—which, since we were at the mall, was probably their target demographic.

Despite their name, they mostly sold merch. You name it: if it was a beloved franchise, they had a bobblehead of it. They didn't have a café, so we had a hold over them there. But only just barely.

And anyways, their whole store smelled like cologne—nice cologne, not the cheap stuff—instead of coffee, so they had that oddly refined air, too.

To my dismay, Ezra's eyes lit up. "They're like your mirror version."

I groaned. "That's a *Star Trek* reference, isn't it?"

I'd grown up primarily on the *Star Trek* series with Sir Patrick Stewart, which had no Spock, but you get references like that when you've hung around in nerdy circles your whole life.

"Yeah. Like, you guys are Spock. They're evil Spock. With a beard."

"So more attractive and mysterious?"

Ezra gave a noncommittal shrug. "Well, I don't know about mysterious but . . . anyways, we should get to work."

I wanted to ask him whether he liked Spock or Evil Spock better, but I closed my mouth. Probably better to drop it.

We entered the store, the cool air-conditioning reminding me of just another thing Of Dice and Decks lacked. The cashier was chatting with a younger couple. One guy probably around Leon's age—early twenties, if I were to guess—was goggling at a whole shelf of specialty D&D dice.

The only employee who wasn't talking to anyone was a woman sitting behind a counter labeled COLLECTIBLES. She had her head slumped against her hand, and she looked us over in a way that suggested the only thing more boring than working here would be talking to us.

Many people had given me that look in life, but I couldn't let it deter me now. I mustered up as much confidence as I had and strode up to her counter.

"Don't ask me if we have anything that's not behind the glass," she warned. "If it's not there, we don't have it."

I couldn't blame her for being grouchy, even if it did somewhat frustrate me. You work in retail for long enough, you understand that she's just saying what every other retail worker is thinking after dealing with enough customers to gather up some real horror stories.

"Right. Thanks . . . Riley?" Ezra read off her name tag, then he cleared his throat. "That's actually not what we're here for."

"Like I said, if it's for something else—"

"We're here because of a customer of yours—of ours, too," I said. "Clive Newton. You know of him?"

Riley narrowed her eyes, and I made a mental note to ask her how she got her eyeliner to look so flawless later. Mine always came out a little too smudgy.

"You work at Of Dice and Decks, don't you? We're not supposed to talk to people from other game shops. We're supposed to ask them to leave."

I glanced nervously at the other cashier, still lost in conversation with what must have been a regular. Ezra, however, betrayed no strong emotion. "I see that you're not asking us, though."

"No," she agreed. "Like I said, we're supposed to. But if my supervisor wanted me to do what he said, then maybe he should pay me more than minimum wage."

I sucked in my cheeks. "That's rough."

"Hmm. Try living on it; see how rough it is then." She drummed her fingers on the countertop. "Why do you care about Clive?"

"I didn't—not more than any other customer." I took a deep breath. "But then he was found dead in front of my shop. And I think I have an obligation to figure out more in case it happens again."

"You mean in case the police start thinking it's you and you end up in jail? I've seen a lot of detective shows. I know how that works."

"Well . . . yes, maybe," I admitted. "But that's only because I'm innocent. I didn't know much of anything about Clive. Nobody at my shop did. I don't know where to begin to look to figure out who's really behind his death, and I don't have much time to do it."

Riley was silent a moment, and then she spoke in a lower voice. "You can't have worked with him that often, or you'd know why we don't let him in the store."

Her words took a few seconds to register, and I still wasn't sure I'd heard her right after they processed. "You don't— you mean he's banned?"

"Is he banned? Of course he is. I've never even seen him in person. I've only heard rumors. But he's not been allowed here for at least as long as I've worked here, and that's been almost six months."

She trailed off and pulled out a flyer from under the counter. "We actually have this sign out front, if you noticed. Randolph made me put it up."

The way she pronounced that name . . . so much hatred. Whoever this Randolph person was, he had to be pretty cruel to deserve that level of wrath.

"He's my supervisor," she said, as if reading my mind. "He thinks he's smart because he's a philosophy major. But I'm a math major, and I know he's just full of hot air."

I took the paper and held it up to my face. There he was— Clive staring down the camera in a way that resembled a Wild West outlaw paper.

"Why are we always behind the times on everything?" I groaned, handing Riley the paper back—which she crumpled up and tossed who-knows-where.

"Okay. So it sounds like he hasn't been here in a while, then," said Ezra. "Do you know anyone else in the collectibles scene we might talk to? Maybe a client, or another collector?"

Riley raised an eyebrow. "Do I look like the kind of person who wastes my time selling dusty old board games to rich lowlifes?"

Ezra frowned. "That depends. What would that sort of person look like, and where would we find them?"

"Stupid. They would look stupid." She shook her head. "Like I said, I just hear things. But there is one person that everyone—at least everyone in this store—knows will buy anything a collector says is valuable. No questions asked."

"Great!" Ezra beamed. "That would at least be a start."

"And if it's such valuable information to you, I'm sure you wouldn't mind grabbing me a mall pretzel?"

"Is that really the way to act about a murder inves—"

"Ben, it's fine." Ezra rubbed my shoulder, leaving goosebumps wherever his fingers touched. "I was going to get pretzels anyways, remember?"

I looked at him. I shook my head. He kept my gaze.

Seven minutes later, we returned with, miraculously, pretzels. Despite my skepticism at finding such a stand, Ezra had a skill for sniffing out delicious, salty carb-laden treats when he was really craving it.

"I included a cheese dipping sauce in there, in case you were looking for a little extra flavor." Ezra handed her the bag gingerly, like it was one of those sack flour babies from seventh-grade home economics. "The pretzel's just original, but I figured you can't go wrong with it!"

"Can we focus," I suggested meekly, holding up my finger, "on finding evidence about the man who got murdered? Even another collector's name would be helpful."

Ezra and Riley both looked at me wordlessly. I had half a mind to ask Ezra whose side he was on: mine, or the Geek

Chic employee he met ten minutes and a pretzel run ago? But the other half of myself didn't want to do anything that would make Ezra annoyed at me, because I secretly preferred it much more when he smiled.

"I like you better," said Riley, turning to Ezra. "So I'll tell you."

"I can still hear you."

"Her name's Madelyn Kerr. She runs a collectibles booth at the annual Salty Con. Has a successful eBay business on the side, from what I've heard."

"As it so happens, we're already planning to visit Salty Con," Ezra said.

"If you find her booth, you might be able to figure something out about Clive. She's a collector we actually let into the store, and they used to work together, from what I've heard."

"And not anymore?"

"No, I think if he weren't already dead, she'd sooner wring his neck than talk to him," mused Riley. "But you'll have to talk to her if you want to know why. It's not my story to tell, nor do I have any interest in doing that."

"I don't suppose you have a phone number for this . . . Madelyn?" said Ezra, grasping in the air with his hand in a perfect mimic at the metaphorical straws he was grasping at.

"No, I don't make friends with customers. It would interrupt my work-life balance, and I'd rather quit than risk that."

She had a point, in such a clear and I'm-younger-and-more-knowledgeable-than-you way, that I couldn't do much except fold my arms.

"And she'll buy . . ." I trailed off. "Anything?"

Riley glanced at something behind us. "As I said, I barely know Madelyn, but I'm sure she's open to it if it means she can cuss out Clive a little. She doesn't strike me as a person that would care much about speaking ill of the dead."

"I'm nothing if not good at—"

"You guys need to go," she said, emphasizing each word. "Now."

My first instinct was to turn around, and I followed it. I regretted it.

Of course I recognized the owner of Geek Chic—Craig Bird. We'd lived in his shadow—literally, since the guy was so tall, he probably just gave people weather forecasts without them asking. His thick, well-styled mustache—which drooped around his face—twitched when he saw me.

And then he started walking towards us.

I began speed-walking for the exit, Ezra close behind me. How did the guy recognize me after, what, fifteen years? I didn't even remember what I looked like at that age.

"Ben Rosencrantz?" he repeated, sounding closer to my ear than I'd have liked. "Don't think I've seen you lurking around lately. Not since the Viggo Mortensen incident."

I didn't answer, my face straight ahead, but Ezra gawked at me in a way that I couldn't ignore.

"Viggo Mortensen? He was here?"

"Of course not," I hissed; then I blushed. "Stole a cardboard cutout of Aragorn. From *Lord of the Rings*?"

"I never knew you were a shoplifter back in the day," said Ezra.

"It wasn't shoplifting. It was a prank. And anyways, everyone should be able to forget one stupid thing they did in high school."

"I don't think I've seen you since high school," interrupted Mr. Bird, folding his arms. "Why now?"

Reluctantly, Ezra and I explained the events of the past few days—some of which he was already familiar with. Sugar House was a fairly small neighborhood, even within a big city, and people tended to talk when something serious happened. But the backpack full of money, he didn't know about—and he seemed to understand my concern as to why that could make me a suspect.

"I didn't know Clive well enough to be of much help," began Mr. Bird. "He wasn't welcome at our shop."

"He wasn't welcome at Ben's shop, either," said Ezra.

"No, I doubt he was." Mr. Bird scratched his head. "I can tell you what little I know about Clive, if that would help you. It really is nice to see you again, Ben. I couldn't help but worry I'd done something to offend you, when you stopped coming to the young men's activities."

"It's appreciated," I said. "And if it's okay . . . can we keep this mostly professional?"

Mr. Bird frowned. "I don't follow."

I took a deep breath. "Every time I run into someone from the old youth group, they want to talk about why I left it. Like if they can fix whatever it is about me that made me leave, I'll come back and their, I don't know, consciences will be alleviated."

"Sure," said Mr. Bird.

"But there's nothing about me to fix. Nothing related to my sexual orientation, anyways." I took a deep breath. "I'm just . . . tired of being treated like a problem, that's all."

"You're not a problem. We can agree on that. So you want to know about Clive, then? Anything would help?"

Ezra and I nodded.

"I haven't seen Clive around our shop in a long time," said Mr. Bird. "But that doesn't surprise me, since I banned him."

"Was there anything in particular that led you to that choice?"

Mr. Bird raised an eyebrow. "Have you been around him for more than two minutes?"

I didn't know whether to speak ill of the dead, but my interactions with Clive had hardly been pleasant.

"He doesn't strike me as trustworthy," I admitted.

"That's an understatement. I'm sad about what happened to him, but I can't say I'm surprised."

"My dad didn't like to do business with him, either."

"Your dad is a smart guy. Clive only seemed to come in with items to sell when he needed the money, and always for much less than they were worth."

"Strange." A thought occurred to me. "Do you think he was stealing them?"

Mr. Bird shrugged. "I wouldn't know about that. I'd think it would have caught up with him if it was. But then again, maybe it did."

"If you weren't buying from him, and my dad wasn't, then where was he getting his money?"

"Oh, private collectors. They're usually a little less scrupulous."

"Any that you know?"

"We don't really sell collectibles at Geek Chic. That's what made it even stranger that he wanted to do business with us. And it's not like this was his full-time job, either. He should have had the sense to find collectors where he'd actually make money."

"Ben's dad mentioned he worked at a computer repair shop," Ezra said. "Do you know anything about the owners?"

"Yes, not far from here. A shop in Holladay. Though I doubt he made much money from that, either."

Holladay was only a few miles away from Sugar House. I could drive over this same afternoon and see if I could ask the owner what they knew about Clive.

"Thanks. We'll have to visit. Maybe they know something more recent about Clive."

"I hope she does, for both of your sake. Ben . . ." Mr. Bird hesitated. "Tell me if I'm overstepping. But what you said about how people see you as a project . . . I'm sorry if I treated you like one, growing up."

I winced.

"Sometimes. But I try not to dwell on the past. I made mistakes then, too. I want to make my present happier."

"I'm glad. After you left Utah, I wondered what had become of you and hoped that you're doing all right. And I'm proud of you, that you are."

"You are?"

"I am. Tell your dad hi for me, okay?"

I nodded.

As Ezra and I left, we discussed our meeting with Mr. Bird and his assistant Riley. While the former hadn't given us much new information, Riley's tip to visit Madelyn Kerr's booth at Salty Con was at least something.

"Holladay's not too far. If you want, we should have time to make a stop to that computer store."

"I don't know if it will lead anywhere, but who knows? Maybe she can lend insight to Clive's personal life."

Ezra nodded. "And you're feeling all right? It sounded like you and Mr. Bird had quite a history."

I sighed. "Sure. He was never unkind to me in an intentional way. It's just a time of life I'd rather not revisit."

"I can understand that," Ezra mused. "It's hard growing up, and you think that you won't belong in the whole world just because you don't in the bubble you were born in. But then when you grow up, you find that the world's a lot bigger, and what you needed was to let the bubble pop."

"I just wish . . ."

What? That Dad would have convinced me not to go to a youth group that every single other kid spent their Tuesday nights at, that was almost essential for making friends? We lived in Utah in the early 2000s. No matter what he or anyone else could have done, I would have never felt like I belonged. The culture was changing and getting better in a lot of ways, but back then, gay marriage wasn't even legal.

"It was a long time ago," I finished. "It doesn't matter. Suffice it to say, I'm glad it's passed."

Chapter 11

Clive's old place of work looked as if it were ripped directly out of the eighties—and not in the aesthetically pleasing, nostalgia-pulling-at-your-heartstrings way. I almost sneezed because of the sheer level of dust in the air. There were still floppy disks on the shelves. Floppy disks.

I mean, sure. Had I found a fourth-edition copy of Dungeons & Dragons among the wares being sold from Dad's inventory at our own shop? Yes. But we capitalized off old geeky stuff. Even if we preferred to stay away from collectibles, plenty of newer items catered to those with nostalgic tastes. Think about it. What would you rather own: some new edition of Clue with rules that made the game more complex but not necessarily better, or one styled to look exactly like the one you had when you were a kid?

Unless you were a collector of old computers—and in that case, you likely already knew how to fix them—you probably weren't looking for a repair shop without even a laptop in sight.

Many buildings in Sugar House looked homey—it was part of the aesthetic—but this one made me feel as if I had literally walked into someone's home. All shelves had stacks of papers—flyers? printer fodder?—jutting off of them at haphazard angles. The carpet had more coffee stains than I was pretty sure health inspectors were supposed to allot public buildings. There was a cat at the foot of one computer (circa 2005, if I were to guess), and it did not look happy we were here.

There were two employees. One, the cashier, looked around high school–aged and more bored than I knew a single person was capable of. His arms, which he was resting his head on, were droopier than a bloodhound with clinical depression's ears.

The other one was a few decades older—around Dad's age or a little older, if I were to guess. Her feet were propped up against one chair, and she was slumped over reading *I.T. Weekly* in the other. Not the one about the celebrities, nor a theoretical one about murderous sewer clowns: the one about troubleshooting computers.

I couldn't quite read her expression, as her transition lenses masked it—but her eyebrows were furrowed in a way that read "irritated, at best."

"Oh! A customer!" The cashier, whose badge read MORGAN, straightened his shoulders and turned to who I presumed was the owner. "What do I do?"

"What do you mean, what do you do? I don't pay you to do anything but check out. After they've found things to check out." As she folded her magazine and set it down, she shook her head. "Kids these days, right? So jittery."

Right beyond her was a drip coffee machine that smelled . . . burnt. I wondered if that had something to do with Morgan's jitteriness?

"Is this a bad time?" Ezra blurted out, then covered his mouth. "Sorry. I just—we can go."

"No, no. Technically, we serve customers."

"Ah, I see. We're not strictly here on business—" When she raised an eyebrow, I backtracked. "Well, we are technically. We'd like to enquire about a man, I believe he was a former employee of yours?"

"Clive," she said flatly, then sat back down and gestured to the other chair. "Sit."

It was more a command, something you would say to a golden retriever. But we obeyed. Somewhat. Ezra and I both stared at the lone chair for a few seconds.

"What? Sit!"

Ezra gestured to me and, not sure what else I really could do, I sat. Ezra stared for a second.

"No, you—" I tried to insist, but he squeezed my shoulder and sat me down in the chair.

Then, he sat on the floor while I tried to hide the blush creeping up on my cheeks like some lovesick teenager. To be fair, though, growing up gay in Utah had probably stunted my romantic growth on some level. So I allowed myself a bit of immaturity and avoided Ezra's eye contact.

"You're not the first person to come asking around about Clive," she said grimly. "A lady—someone with the cops, I think—came here this morning."

The coffee mug in her hands was steaming, even though I hadn't noticed her make a cup. I looked at it and wondered if she would make me one if I asked nicely. Probably not. Maybe if I started crying, but my tear ducts were so dry lately.

"Oh?"

"I turned her away." She leaned her head back and downed the cup in several gulps. "Told her I had my rights. I don't know if that's true or not, if you can turn the cops away like that, but it worked on her."

"Are you going to do the same with us?" asked Ezra.

She scrutinized us both, an unreadable expression on her face. She snorted and set the coffee cup on the ground. At least a stain would immortalize this meeting.

"No. No, I don't think so. I'll tell you what I know. Heaven knows if it's useful."

"Why not?"

In response, she got up and pulled a DVD case off the shelf. She handed it to Ezra.

"You look like him."

We both looked at the cover. It was a children's PC game from at least a generation ago, and it depicted an anthropomorphic slime ball surfing. With sunglasses on. It also had a goatee.

"I'm . . . what?" said Ezra.

"No, not him. Sorry." She flipped it over, and on the back was a man who looked a lot like Ezra if he had come of age in the seventies. "My husband Ralph was a game developer. He . . . he passed on last April. Stomach cancer ran in his family, but he was always too stubborn to get an endoscopy. Said things would turn out or they wouldn't, and either way we'd be all right."

She wiped her face with her sleeve, frowning. "Allergies coming earlier and earlier every year. They give the plants here too much fertilizer for their own good."

"I'm truly sorry to hear that," said Ezra softly.

"Don't be. I'm the one who over-fertilizes them. Print's too small."

Morgan cleared his throat, then pretended to be wiping the counter when she looked over.

"I'm Jamie," she said, extending her hand and then pocketing it after wavering between Ezra and me for a few seconds. "Jamie Farnsworth, if you want to write that down. And yes, Clive did work here. Some might say unfortunately."

"Would you?" I asked, and then mouthed to Ezra while she wasn't looking, "Should we be writing things down?"

He shrugged, then got his phone out from his pocket and tapped on the "Memos" app.

"Eh. He was a terrible employee, so I guess so. But his

mom and I used to scrapbook together when our kids were young, so what can you do?"

I imagined Clive as a rosy-cheeked, undoubtedly loud little boy. His first steps. Him performing in his elementary school play, maybe as Angry Rock #3. I guess it never occurred to me that he was someone's child.

I tried not to think about that. It made my heart ache in a way that felt strange for someone who had insulted me multiple times and then inadvertently framed me for murder.

"That must have been hard for you," said Ezra. He reached out, as if to put his palm over hers in comfort, then thought better of it and patted my knee.

"It was. It was hard keeping him employed when all he'd do was log into our Wi-Fi and look at stupid video game cheat codes. And it was hard when he died, of course."

"Ah."

"Barbara's his mother. Or was, though I don't know if you ever stop being a mother even after you die. She was in a nursing home not too far from here, actually, until recently. Unfortunately, she passed away, or I'd arrange a meeting between you two."

"Was he . . ." I searched for the right word. "Acting strangely? In the days before he died, I mean?"

"He's—or he was—a strange person. Always leaving his shift to feed his cat, but I know it died at least five years ago." She exhaled slowly. "And then there were the Googles."

"Excuse me?"

"The Googles," Jamie said impatiently. "He had been Googling weird things before his death. I told you, I monitor the Internet history here like I'm a security guard. Every day as I eat my dinner. It's my favorite hobby."

Morgan caught my eye and nodded with a grim certainty, then busied himself with a computer magazine.

"I don't want to speak ill of the . . . I mean, Clive was an idiot. But he was my idiot. And I really didn't think about it at the time. I thought he was just looking up inane theoreticals. He does that most days."

"Please," I said. "If you know anything that might point to an answer, maybe it could help us find whoever killed him."

She hesitated; then, with a glance to Ezra, said, "Things like, 'how to fake your own death.' "

The three of us were silent as goosebumps prickled up on my arms. It was as if R.L. Stine himself had walked in wiggling his fingers and going, "Oooh, so scary, isn't it . . . buy my books."

I then listed that under *intrusive thoughts to tell my therapist about* in my brain.

"But . . . but that was him. At least, I think it was him. It was someone, at least." I rubbed my temples. "He doesn't have a twin?"

"Oh, no. He has a younger brother, but they're not close. Nor do they look identical."

"And they've only learned how to clone sheep so far, right?" said Ezra.

"I don't know," said Jamie. "Probably not people, no. Not that fast. He also Googled, 'does the transporter in *Star Trek* kill you every time you use it, or does it transport your soul, too,' so maybe he was just having a weird week."

Ah, yes. I'd Googled that many times, too, with increasing agitation, but now didn't seem like a good time to mention that.

"Anything else?"

"No, nothing else. Otherwise, he was pretty much regular Clive. Loud as a bear. Smelly also as a bear. Regular Clive."

There didn't seem to be anything in her tone that suggested she really meant "irregular Clive," so I started to stand up. "Thank you for your time, Jamie."

"Of course. Barbara knew him better than me, but I'm happy to help where I can."

"If I can ask, why didn't you tell the police? You seem eager to find out whatever happened to Clive."

"Oh, that's an easy one." She smiled tightly, but it didn't meet her eyes. "My ex—this was before Ralph—was an investigator-for-hire. The kind that followed people who their spouses suspected were cheating. Which made it ironic, when . . . well, let's just say I'm a sentimental woman."

Chapter 12

❧

Clive's family held the funeral at a local Latter-day Saints chapel, no more than a twenty-minute drive from Dad's house. It was easy to find, not only due to the grid system Salt Lake County roads operated on, but because Mormon churches followed a similar design structure.

Most of them were flat and rectangular, with a white steeple jutting up on the side closest to the road. If you took the highway, you could play a game that had become the pastime of many bored Utahn kids called "Count the Churches."

My record? Forty-six.

Ezra and I sat in the back of the auditorium, in the metal overflow chairs that grated against the linoleum.

Not that they needed it. The church was sparsely populated with mourners, no more than a few per row. But I figured that the pews were for family and friends, and I already felt like I was intruding on something Ezra and I shouldn't have been invited to.

As the opening prayer began, I closed my eyes and folded my arms. I began to shake. All I could picture as the church bishop gave his remarks was Clive's body bleeding out in front of our shop.

Maybe this hadn't been such a good idea. Discomfort, I expected to find at Clive's funeral, but not pure panic.

"Ben," whispered Ezra, "are you all right?"

My mouth dry, I answered, "I . . . think I need to sit in the hall."

I stood up, as quiet as I could be, and moved down the rows and out the exit.

In the front lobby, there were two floral-patterned couches, presumably for people to sit down on in between sermons. I sat down on one and hunched over, putting my hand on my forehead.

I took a few breaths to steady myself, then tensed when I felt a hand on my shoulder.

"If you need to go, just say the word."

I hadn't known Ezra had followed me out. I didn't want him to see me like this. I turned away, and he lowered his hand away—and immediately, I missed the touch.

"No," I finally said. "I'll be all right. I promise. It's just . . . been a lot to handle, that's all."

"You don't look fine at all. You're shaking."

I straightened up, held out a hand in front of me.

"It just brought back memories I didn't expect. I haven't been here in a while." I stood up. "We should go back in. I might not have known Clive, but the least we can do is try to gather—"

"If you didn't know Clive," said a new voice, "then can I ask what you're doing at his funeral?"

A man wearing a purple fleur-de-lis tie with his black blazer and slacks stood by the auditorium doors. His hair, of which there was very little, stuck up in tufts like a duck's bottom. He was smirking, and had lines around his face that suggested he spent a lot of his time smirking.

"Luncheon delivery?" Ezra suggested.

"Nice try. The great-aunts made all the ham and funeral potatoes this morning."

"Hello," I said, as it was the only thing I could think to say while so flustered. "We're just here to pay our respects."

I hoped, as he strode forward and scrutinized me, that my face wasn't as flushed as it felt.

"You're speaking to his brother," said the man. "The least you could do is give me a name."

My throat went tight as I remembered Leon's warning. If Clive hadn't had such a great relationship with his brother, then perhaps this man was dangerous.

"I saw you and your husband leave the auditorium, and I couldn't place your face," said the man. "It made me wonder if you were a friend of Clive's. He never had many. My brother was a hard man to love."

I waited for Ezra to correct the mistake Clive's brother made—that we were colleagues, not married—but he didn't say anything. He seemed to be watching my reaction.

"I'm sorry to say that I didn't know him as well as my dad." I hesitated. "We own a board game shop, and Clive was one of our regulars."

"That was certainly his passion, wasn't it?" Clive's brother cocked his head to the side. "And perhaps his downfall. But I'm not one for gossip."

"I grew up in the business, and I didn't know board games could attract so many enemies."

"If they're valuable enough, why not? If playing them makes people competitive, owning them can make them violent." Clive's brother pointed at me, as if trying to place me. "You said your dad owns a board game shop?"

"He does."

"Would it happen to be the one where my brother was found?"

Dang it. While trying to be vague, I had accidentally made it even worse for myself. I might have done better to just give him my name and thrown in my Social Security number while I was at it.

"He was. On the, uh, porch, to be specific," I hedged. "But I promise we had nothing to do with it."

"Oh, I believe you," said Clive's brother. "Murderers never return to the scene of the crime. Or isn't that what people say?"

I had always heard the opposite, but it didn't seem in my best interest to correct him.

"Ben wouldn't hurt a rat, even if it gave him the plague," said Ezra. "In fact, he's trying to help the police get leads."

Clive's brother turned to me. "You are?"

I exchanged glances with Ezra and nodded. Whether it was such a good idea to tell Clive's brother this when we weren't so sure he hadn't put the knife in Clive's chest, I didn't know.

"Then it sounds like your reasons for attending the service weren't so selfless as you say, were they?" Clive's brother mused. "Sounds to me as if you're trying to get yourself out of hot water."

My hands started to shake again, so I shoved one in my pocket.

"Boiling," I admitted.

Clive's brother considered the two of us. "What's your name?"

"Ben."

"I'll help you, Ben, if I can. My brother and I weren't exactly close, but perhaps I have information that could be of use to you."

"Why would you do that?" I asked.

"Because I'm doing it on one condition." Clive's brother's smirk widened. "You own a board game shop? Prove it. Beat me in a game of Liar's Dice, and I'll tell you anything you ask."

I looked around. To play Liar's Dice, each player needed at least six dice and a small cup to hide them from the other players.

"Here?"

"No, no, not here." Clive's brother pulled out his phone,

tapped furtively on it, and handed it to me. "At my home. It's been so long since I've taken my set out. I'll need to dust it."

I added my phone number and name to his contacts, figuring that he could track me down if he wanted to just fine at this point, and handed it back to him.

"I don't know if it's a great idea for us to go alone to your home."

"Who said anything about us, Ben?" said Clive's brother. "It'll be you versus me."

"What if I lose?"

"Then you go home," said Clive's brother, "and do whatever it is people do before they get charged for a murder they didn't commit. Sulk, maybe?"

"I've done enough sulking." I weighed my options. Both seemed heavy enough to drag me to the bottom of despair. "All right. Just one game?"

"Until only one is left with dice in their cup." Clive's brother put his phone back in his pocket and made his way back to the auditorium. "I'll text you the address. Let's say Sunday afternoon?"

"Wait!" When Clive's brother turned around, I said, "You didn't give us your name. What was it?"

Clive's brother's nose scrunched up. "Mr. Newton, thank you. Be seeing you, Mr. Rosencrantz."

The door's thud echoed in the hallway behind him.

"Ben?" said Ezra. "I'm going with you. I don't like the idea of you going to his house at all, but you're not going alone."

"I agree," I said. "I don't know if we can trust that guy. I doubt we can."

"Not when he's trying to gamble evidence that he says could help solve Clive's murder," agreed Ezra. "But maybe we can catch him in a lie. That could be useful to us, too. Maybe."

"Maybe," I said.

I felt faint and needed to sit down again. Between the conversation, the occasion, and the setting, I was drained.

"You really don't look well," Ezra fretted. "Have you eaten today?"

"I was hoping there'd be funeral potatoes at the luncheon," I muttered. "What good is going to a Mormon church if there aren't funeral potatoes."

"Well, we came here to find a lead. And we got one, right?"

"There could be more. Maybe we should stay."

"If we interview every single person here, not only will they be traumatized, but you'll be, too." Ezra grabbed my hand and helped me to my feet. "Let me cook you something. We can work more on the case tomorrow, but to do that, you need rest and food."

Ezra's apartment was close to downtown Salt Lake City, little more than an hour's drive in rush hour traffic. His living room was tidy, and though many plants lined the window ("Mostly herbs," he'd said. "I like to keep simpler plants at home"), they seemed well taken care of.

He led me to the couch and patted one of the throw pillows. "You rest, all right? I mean it."

"I can help," I protested. "I'm not a total waste in the kitchen."

He folded his arms. "What's the last thing you cooked on your own?"

It took some effort, but I thought about what I'd made myself for dinner the night before.

"Macaroni and cheese."

"Frozen meal or actual macaroni and cheese?"

"Dad got a tool to make crustless sandwiches," I said, rather than answer him. "Like a large peanut butter and jelly bread ravioli. I made myself three of those for lunch yesterday. Does that count?"

"No, Ben. That counts even less." Ezra pinched the bridge

of his nose. "I'll repeat myself, then. You rest. I can take care of this."

To his point, I didn't know how much I could offer in the kitchen beyond "mild hindrance." And I felt exhausted. Attending Clive's funeral had emotionally drained me, and I gave myself a headache trying to make sense of whatever his brother wanted.

The couch cushions were comfortable enough on my back to slip into something between asleep and waking. And Ezra's clattering about in the kitchen relaxed me, a background noise I could slip into and feel safe while sleeping against.

At some indeterminate time in the future, the doorbell woke me up. I lifted my head blearily. Ezra, more panicked than he had been before I'd fallen asleep but still in the kitchen, drew a line across his neck.

I cocked my head to the side. "Who's that?"

"Could be one of two people," he said. "Detective Shelley, or the missionaries."

"Missionaries," I repeated. "You don't mean . . ."

Mormon missionaries came a pair a neighborhood (at least) in Utah, something I'd never found practical. Every single person in the state knew what Mormonism was. Either they *were* Mormons and had no need of conversion, or they wanted nothing to do with it. Why bother knocking on someone's door to tell them about something they already had a strong opinion about?

"Unfortunately, I do," said Ezra, with the grimness of a queer man with incredibly dense neighbors. "They've been visiting. And visiting. And visiting. I don't know how to scare them off."

I thought back to what Dad and I would do when I was growing up in Sugar House. Whenever they would invite him to church, Dad would politely invite them to join him at his

Unitarian Universalist congregation. As far as I knew, it was rare that anyone took him up on it.

The knocking continued.

"Maybe if we hold still," said Ezra in a low voice, "and stay quiet, they will go away. Remind me, is it Mormons or dinosaurs who can't see objects that don't move?"

"I think we should answer it," I said. "In case it's Detective Shelley. Maybe she saw us at Clive's funeral. Wouldn't it be suspicious if we didn't answer the door?"

Ezra looked longingly at the pot simmering on his stove, then back at the door. "If anything burns, I swear to . . . well, you know."

He took off his oven mitts. The apron stayed on as he strode over to the door and opened it. I stood.

"Elders," he said flatly. "What a surprise. Didn't you just come by last Saturday?"

Well, damn. Pardon the swear, elders.

It was rare that I saw Ezra approach a situation without at least a little curiosity. His shoulders were stiff, blocking the two tie-clad missionaries from seeing much into his apartment.

"Hello, Ezra!" said the one on the left, distinguishable by his horn-rimmed glasses and his name tag, which read MORTENSON. "If you remember, we invited you to the ward potluck, and you said you'd think about it. Well, we're on our way right now and figured we'd stop by to pick you up."

"Who's this, your roommate?" said the one on the right, whose last name was apparently HYDE—something I would have much preferred to do rather than acknowledge his question—and who was holding a tinfoil-covered tray of something that smelled cheesy. "You're welcome, too! We have funeral potatoes. And ham." Ah, there they were. I knew we'd get funeral potatoes somehow with Mormons involved.

"Tempting," said Ezra. "Unfortunately, I—"

"He has a date," I said quickly, before I could really think about it. "With me. His boyfriend. I'm Ben."

Both missionaries and Ezra stared at me in shock. Even I didn't know quite what compelled me to say it. Maybe it was some lingering lightheadedness from the stress of attending the funeral. Or maybe it was my interest to avoid conversations in which people were trying to convert me to something.

Then, Ezra slung his arm around my shoulder with a casualness that I found impressive, as much as I could form thoughts at all. As if he did this dozens of times a day. His fingers traced around my shoulder.

Often, when I brushed against people, I flinched. Especially after Shane and I split up. I'd been on a few dates, most of them organized by whatever dating app I'd been lonely enough to download the weekend before. But when my date clasped his hand around mine, I always drew back.

Maybe it had just been too long, but his touch was welcome.

"I've already cancelled our last date," Ezra said after a few seconds. "I'd be in pretty hot water if I cancelled this one, too."

"Also, we're Unitarian Universalist," I added.

Technically, just Dad was, but I figured if there was a God, He'd let it slide if I lied about religion just this once if it meant getting out of a social event. What was life about, if not that?

"Gotcha," said Elder Mortenson slowly, as if he did not fully get it. "We'll leave you to your evening, Ezra. Nice to meet you, Ben."

"Thank you for your time. You know, we really respect your . . ."

His companion trailed off, searching for a word that just evaded his grasp.

"Community," he finished.

I smiled despite any sentiment beyond politeness urging me to do so. "Thank you very much, elders. Safe travels."

After we shut the door, Ezra turned around and slid slowly against the wall until his butt hit the floor.

"They 'respect our community'?" he repeated. "What does that even mean? Every individual queer person in the whole world?"

"I didn't out you, did I?" I said suddenly. "I didn't even think about that. It was just the first thing that popped into my mind to get them to leave us alone. I'm sorry."

Ezra snorted. "That's very considerate, but I'm not closeted. You're welcome to tell whoever you want. Was it okay that I . . ."

He mimicked reaching his arm out around my shoulder.

"Thank goodness," I said. "I'd be surprised if they visited you much more after that. And yes, that was . . . just fine."

It varied, of course, but missionaries didn't tend to bother gay couples. I liked to think it was out of respect but knew a lot of it probably came down to practicality. It would be hard to convert someone to a religion, after all, that one couldn't be baptized into unless they divorced their spouse.

"That would be nice. I have better things to do than stand at the doorstep turning them away every week. And I'm sure they do, too."

As an afterthought, Ezra said, "I'd be lucky to have you as a boyfriend, anyways."

"Boyfriend?" I repeated, as if the words hadn't come out of my own mouth several minutes earlier.

"Sure," he said. "I could bring you home flowers, and you could read me your English papers. What more do you need in a relationship?"

The thought was tempting. Shane hadn't been interested in my studies. Though to be fair, I hadn't been very interested in his court cases. We didn't often talk about each other's days, over dinner or otherwise.

"Are you sure? All the papers I've written are literary theory," I said. "I wouldn't want to bore you to sleep."

Ezra grinned. "I have insomnia, Ben. Even the boring parts would be fine."

Twenty or so minutes later, Ezra presented me with a plate of pasta with cherry tomatoes and a salty, cheesy sauce; I made borderline-obscene noises while I ate, hunched over a bowl on the couch.

"I'm sorry," I said in between bites. "It's been a long time since I've eaten something this good."

Ezra waved me off from the cushion next to me. "It's just mizithra and butter. Anyone could make it."

"Not true. I couldn't. And you're spoiling my taste buds. Soon they're going to start expecting good food, and then what will I do with myself?"

"Come by more often," said Ezra. "We'll have to keep up appearances for the missionaries, after all. You know . . ."

"Yes?"

"Kit's brewery is holding a pub trivia night next Friday. If you're not busy, perhaps we could go. I don't know anything that would keep the missionaries away more than beer and the appearance of a queer date."

"But how would they know?"

"I was thinking in more of an 'apple a day' kind of way," he said. "Only if you want to, of course. And only as friends. I know dating must be the furthest thing from your mind right now."

It was a lot less far than he might think, being around him, but he was right. Between the murder investigation and the divorce finalized less than a year ago, it was simpler to stay friends.

"Next Friday it is," I said. "Let's call it, in all appearances, a date."

Chapter 13

※

On Sunday, Ezra drove me to the address Mr. Newton gave us in my car. I was feeling a little too weak to drive—not physically, but emotionally. It was starting to occur to me that maybe going to a strange man's home, when it was possible he either knew something about or was Clive's killer, wasn't my best-thought-out idea.

Clive's brother lived in a wealthier Draper neighborhood half an hour outside downtown Salt Lake City. In Salt Lake County, housing prices tended to go up the higher you were on the side of the mountain and the harder it was to get to your home in the winter. Clive's home was up a particularly unwieldy road, one that required a lot of concentration out of Ezra to drive up without tumbling down either side of it.

So it was clear, unfortunately for us, that Mr. Newton had money.

"Do you want me to come inside with you? I could be your Bootstrap Bill."

"It's been a long time since I've seen *Pirates of the Caribbean*," I said. "Do they play Liar's Dice in it?"

"They did," said Ezra, "and Bootstrap Bill was the one who saved Will Turner's life when he almost bet his soul. I can do that for you, too. If things go south, I can take the loss, and maybe he'll still tell you something."

I laughed before I could catch myself, more out of surprise. "I don't need a Bootstrap Bill."

Ezra raised an eyebrow. "Only a concierge, then?"

"All right. You can come in if you want, but I don't know why you would."

"Oh, Ben, don't worry yourself. I've played Ace Attorney."

"You've what?"

"It's another detective game. You are an attorney, and you ask questions to murder suspects and solve the crimes. I do pretty well at it, too. I only have to look up cheats sometimes. Hang on!"

Ezra jogged around the side of the car and opened the passenger door.

"Thank you."

Ezra rang the doorbell after we trudged up the driveway. After a few seconds, we heard a tinny voice come out of the speaker.

"Ben Rosencrantz? Here to claim your gauntlet?"

I gulped. "Yes, it is. How did you know?"

"Camera in the doorbell."

I heard Ezra mutter under his breath, "James Bond–level bullsh—"

"I heard that," said the doorbell. "Who is that, Ben? I didn't say you could bring anyone."

"That's Ezra," I said. "You remember him from the funeral, right? He's my . . . friend?"

I glanced at Ezra. He nodded encouragingly.

The voice took a few moments to respond.

"I see. You've brought yourself a Watson. Shame neither of you seem to fill Sherlock's shoes. He can come in, but he can't play."

"Fine by me," I said.

Ezra groaned. "I haven't played in so long. I was looking forward to it."

"I'll play it with you another time."

"Really?"

"Sure," I said hurriedly. "If you want. But right now, let's just do what Mr. Newton—"

The doorknob turned, and behind the oak frame was Mr. Newton.

"Fancy seeing you here," he said, looking down his nose at us. "Metaphorically fancy, I mean. Is that a Hollister logo on your shirt? You could sell that as a vintage if it wasn't worth pennies."

"There's no need to be so hostile," said Ezra.

"I think I can talk to the prime suspect in my brother's murder however I like."

"If you think I did it," I said, "why invite me over?"

"Oh, I don't, Ben," said Mr. Newton. "But it does feel nice to have someone to direct frustration at. It used to be Clive, but I'm not too keen on speaking ill of the dead."

He let us into the hallway. The usual Utah prints hung on the walls. Scenes from scriptures, both of the Biblical sort and some I didn't recognize that must have been from the Book of Mormon. Though judging by those brushstrokes, these were more than prints.

"Take off your shoes," he said, "then I'll lead you to the dining room. Can I get you something to drink? Mountain Dew? Diet Mountain Dew?"

"Do you have Mountain Dew Zero?" Ezra joked.

Mr. Newton gave him a steely glare. "If you're not going to respect our game, you can leave."

Ezra looked down at the floor. "Water's fine, thank you."

Barefooted and fighting to disregard the pit in my stomach that would row a boat down the street scraped against the gravel if it was the only way to leave this man's house, I followed him into the dining room.

It was a spare place. Six chairs around a custom-made gaming table. And on the table was a Liar's Dice set: two flat, shallow cups and within them, six dice each.

"Take a seat. Anywhere you want."

The room echoed.

Ezra and I sat next to each other. I scooted my chair as close to him as possible, closer than I normally would, until we were as close as you can get without touching. Something about his nearness was calming to my heart, kept it from shredding itself from the inside with its racing.

"Shall we?" said Mr. Newton as he took his seat, sliding a glass of water to Ezra that he ignored.

"I can't do this," I murmured.

"Sometimes when I'm scared," said Ezra, "I try to think of scarier things I've gone through before."

Coming out to my dad came to mind. I winced, but it eased some of the jitteriness.

"Are you thinking of anything right now?" I said.

He considered this. "I was in a community improv troupe, once."

"Scarier than this?"

"At least it's less of a joke," he said. "Does he roll first or you?"

Without breaking eye contact, Mr. Newton and I began shaking our dice cups at the same time. The sound echoed in the dining room like dozens of skeletons playing their ribs like a xylophone.

"At the same time," I grunted.

Both of us slammed our cups onto the table (myself praying that I didn't scratch it, as it looked worth more than the whole game shop). I held my hand around the back of my cup to keep Mr. Newton from seeing.

I took a peek. Of my five dice, four had landed on the number two. One was a five. With Liar's Dice, the more multiples of a number you rolled, the better. This gave you an advantage with your guesses, especially in two-player games.

I kept my expression as unreadable as possible, furrowing

my brow to seem confused. My hope was that if I just played stupid, Mr. Newton would assume the simplest answer.

"Do you want to start the bet?" I asked.

"Please, guest first."

I took a deep breath, closing my eyes. I pictured my happy place: springtime at a duck pond. Beans and I sat under a tree. She basked in the sun while I attempted to read *Dune*. I loved attempting to read *Dune*. It was so much easier to accomplish than actually finishing it.

I counted to five and opened my eyes.

"I think there's at least a single one on the table," I said in a measured voice.

"If you're going to play like a coward, this won't be fun." When I didn't respond, he added, "Two fives."

"Three twos."

"*Four* twos."

He was goading me into raising it, exactly as I wanted him to. Thank goodness I had no real social circle in high school and played board games with the librarian during lunch. I knew that would one day play into my favor. Definitely.

"Five twos," I said.

"No way." Mr. Newton made a beckoning gesture with his hand. "Let me see your dice."

We unveiled our cups at the same time, and he swore.

"Careful, Mr. Newton," said Ezra. "I don't think your hallway paintings would like you using that language."

I checked his dice. There, on his end of the table, lay dice facing up with a variety of numbers, but most importantly, a two. Exactly what I needed to win this round.

He set aside one dice. That was what gave Liar's Dice its edge. Every time you lost a round, you also lost one dice to play on your hand. The more you lost, the harder it would be to make informed guesses.

"Maybe I overestimated you," he said. "Or maybe dumb luck was on your side that round."

"Or maybe," said Ezra, "Ben literally owns a board game shop."

"Then it will be even more embarrassing when he loses." Mr. Newton shook his dice cup with increased vigor and slammed it onto the table. "Round two, let's go."

This time around, I got no matching numbers. I glanced up at Mr. Newton. He was smirking, but I supposed that could mean any number of things. Maybe he rolled in his favor. Maybe he was just trying to intimidate me. Maybe he was just a jerk.

Most likely a combination of the three was the answer.

"I'll start the guesses this time." Mr. Newton drummed his fingers on the table. "How about . . . four sixes."

I bit my cheek. He was forcing my hand into either calling him out or raising the bet to an unreasonable number. And while I had gotten four twos last time, my hand this round was less promising. I only had one six on my end. The question was, how many did he have?

"Five sixes?"

"Absolutely not."

He raised his hand. Only one six lay scattered below his cup. He'd been bluffing after all.

I took a dice from my hand and set it aside.

The next three rounds were equally shameful, considering this wasn't my first or even fiftieth game of Liar's Dice. I just couldn't seem to get into this guy's head. Two dice gone, then three, then four.

"Looks like we're four to one," said Mr. Newton. "There's no shame in giving up. I've gotten all I wanted out of this."

"And what did you want from it?" I snapped, despite myself.

Mr. Newton said nothing. He shook his dice cup and set it on the table.

"When you're ready," he said.

Ezra squeezed my shoulder as I shook my dice—perhaps for the last time—and slammed my cup down. I lifted the top just a crack, but I didn't look in.

"One five," I said.

"One five, you think?" Mr. Newton tented his fingers, leaning back in his chair. "Two fives."

"No."

We lifted our cups. My dice turned out to be a three. Only one of his was a five.

He scowled, and he continued scowling through the next two rounds. I pretended to peek at my dice, kept my voice calm, and bluffed my way into knocking off two more of his dice.

One to one. The final round.

"All I want is a conversation," I said. "You've got to understand. My career and maybe even my life is on the line. Maybe something you know could help me find the real killer."

"And you've got to understand that I hate talking about my brother." We shook our dice and set them on the table one last time. He peered at his, his face blank. "This has been fun, Ben, but I do have things to do today. One four."

I gritted my teeth. Without meaning to, or even thinking about it consciously, I looked down at my dice.

A four looked back up at me. Could we really have the same number? I couldn't call him out, and I didn't want to risk throwing out a number at random.

"Two fours."

As soon as I saw Mr. Newton's grin, my chest sank.

"Nope."

He lifted his cup and called my bluff. On his end, his single dice was faced up at the number one.

"It's all right, Ben," murmured Ezra. "This guy's full of it. I doubt he knows anything."

Mr. Newton clapped his hands but, after a moment, his face fell. "Oh, it wasn't even a satisfying victory. I could read your partner's face most of the time. For the sake of your savings, never get into poker."

"Is that where you made enough to support all this?" I said, gesturing around to his spacious home.

He chuckled, a hollow sound made even more so by the acoustics in this room. "Not through it. More in spite of it. It's . . . how I cope, I guess you can say."

Ezra and I exchanged glances. Mr. Newton sank back in his chair. He sighed.

"It started," said Mr. Newton, "with our mother."

Ezra pulled out his phone from his pocket and held it under the table. He pressed "record," just as I had seen so many college freshmen do in my Survey of Shakespeare course that they'd mistakenly thought would be a pushover elective because they'd watched *The Lion King* once.

"Well, no, that's not quite true," said Mr. Newton. "Really, it began with our names."

"Yours and Clive's?" Ezra prompted.

Mr. Newton opened his mouth, thought better of it, and then nodded.

"Our mom was a high school seminary teacher for the Mormon church," he said. "And there was one author she loved more than anyone else. One author with the most unfortunate name that she decided to inflict on her two sons, one after the other."

Ezra's brow furrowed while I felt a mounting pit of dread in my stomach. I'd spent enough time at the library as a child to know where this was going. Surely a parent couldn't be so oblivious, so unintentionally cruel.

"Of course you've heard of C.S. Lewis," said Mr. Newton. "It is Utah, after all. Half of the population worships him because they're nerds and the other half because they're spiritual."

"C.S. Lewis's first name was Clive?" said Ezra. "Clive Lewis? That's not too bad. Why the C.S.?"

"Wait until you hear his middle name," said Mr. Newton grimly. "And my first."

"Please, for the love of all that is good," I begged, "tell me your parents didn't name you Staples."

Without being able to help himself, Ezra burst out in a peal of giggles.

"Sorry," I said, while Ezra tried to gasp the same.

"Don't spare my feelings. The kids at school never did. My mom never considered that kids don't care about the legacy of C.S. Lewis. They used to pelt packs of staples they'd stolen from the teacher at my head, shouting, 'Staples for Staples! Staples for Staples!' And you know who never stopped them? Clive."

Mr. Newton clenched his hand into a fist. I pulled out my own phone under the table and tapped a note with one hand.

Mr. Newton—residual anger toward brother? Enough to kill or normal sibling rivalry?

"Our childhood was mediocre, but Clive's was somewhat less so. He was born first, so he got the normal name. And Mom's love. Dad was ambivalent about both of us, but at least Clive had Mom." Mr. Newton played with the dice on the table, arranging them into a pyramid. "I never fit in with those two. I tried, but I just couldn't get myself to care about inane fantasy worlds like them. Not when I already found that in economics."

"Curse those inane fantasy worlds," said Ezra.

"Indeed. They went to all of the *Star Trek* midnight movie showings together. Mom even skipped work the next day to go with him. But when I graduated salutatorian of the Marriott Business School? Nothing. Barely even a mention. Sent me a gift card for Olive Garden on the day of my graduation ceremony. I lived in his nerdy shadow, and I hated it."

He knocked over his dice pyramid with a flick. One hit Ezra in the forearm. He gasped but said nothing—perhaps feeling ashamed of laughing earlier.

"And then there was the matter of inheritance," said Mr. Newton. "When Mom died, she left most of her belongings to Clive—on the belief that he would share what he could with me if I needed it. Clive never did as well financially as I did, so I suppose her reasoning made sense in her mind. But he cut off contact with me as soon as we didn't have Mom to keep us together. I've asked for a few keepsakes to remember her by, even knocked on his door a few times to beg or offer money—I'm not proud. But never so much as drew the curtains to look at me."

While nodding and making an empathetic sound, I added to my note, *Definitely abnormal.*

"So you see, Clive and I were 'estranged.' To put it lightly. If you really want to know about Clive's last days, I know where I would go. I'd ask his only friend. Or the only one that I know of, anyways. Emmett Acevedo. It's like I said. After Mom died, Clive and I hardly talked."

"I hope you don't take this the wrong way," said Ezra, "but why waste our time with this whole game?"

"I'm sorry. Did you have Emmett's name before? No, you didn't? Then maybe what you should be saying is 'thanks.' " Mr. Newton looked down. "It has been a while since I played a game without any money on the line. It was . . . fine."

"There are people who come and play together at Of Dice and Decks," I said hesitantly. "If you promise not to scare off my customers, I won't bother you if you come by."

Mr. Newton studied me. Something flickered behind his eyes, but he masked whatever it was right away.

"Emmett Acevedo," he repeated. "He's a professor at Westminster College. Humanities, I believe. He and Clive had a . . . tempestuous friendship, you could say. You might get somewhere by asking why he bothered hanging around with Clive at all when he was treated so terribly, the times I was around them."

I made another quick note of Emmett's name on my phone, then shoved it into my pocket.

"How long ago was the last you talked to Clive?" I asked.

"Around when Mom passed away. A year ago, maybe? I heard it was unceremonious."

We thanked him (out of courtesy more than anything else) and left.

"That was unexpected of you."

"What?"

Ezra's voice startled me out of my reverie staring outside of the car window.

"Telling Staples—I mean, Mr. Newton—that he can visit the shop. I don't think I would have said that."

I rubbed the back of my neck. "Well, we could always use more business. And I think underneath the rudeness, he must be a little lonely."

"That's not what I meant. You aren't worried that he murdered Clive?"

"Oh! Right." I smacked the top of my head. "Great. I invited a possible murderer into my shop."

"All might not be lost," said Ezra. "At least you could keep a closer eye on him if he does start hanging around."

"I'll have to if he does. I don't want to get too comfortable and, I don't know, get a crowbar shoved down my throat."

"That sounds unpleasant," agreed Ezra. "At least Westminster isn't too far from your old stomping grounds. Maybe you can pull the colleague card and set up a meeting."

"I don't know. If he and Clive had a messy breakup, he might not be too keen to talk." I paused. "But I've got to talk to him. I barely knew Clive. I need an insider's perspective."

Plus, Westminster wasn't too far from Of Dice and Decks— a mile's walk, if that. I could go during my lunch break and hardly be missed at the shop.

"You'll be safe, right?" Ezra glanced away from the road for just a second. "I can come with you again."

I shook my head. "If I know anything, I know academia. Too well, unfortunately. I'll try and set up an appointment with Professor Acevedo, see where it leads."

Chapter 14

✺

"Mr. Rosencrantz," said Detective Shelley. "The sunglasses really aren't necessary."

I took the offending shades off and put them in my shirt pocket. "You're sure? I don't want anyone bad to spot us."

Detective Shelley frowned. "Ben."

"Yes?" I said, startled at her use of my first name—so far, she seemed to have disregarded my indication that I preferred it.

"This is a Starbucks."

Indeed it was, and a fairly sleepy one, considering how most people were here this early in the morning to get caffeinated. I usually got my morning drinks from Sophie's café, but Detective Shelley had agreed to meet me here for a discussion before Of Dice and Decks opened.

"I know that. But I want to be safe. Nobody has been arrested for Clive's murder, right?"

"No." Detective Shelley studied her cold brew, tilted her head back, and downed most of it in a few gulps. She set the cup back down on the table, resigned. "I suppose you didn't call me for a simple check-in?"

"Not simple, but I think it's helpful."

"Have any more strange items been left at your home or storefront?"

"No, and I hope none do. But I've been doing a little research of my own."

Detective Shelley narrowed her eyes. "Have you, Mr. Rosencrantz?"

"Yes. In my free time. And I think I may have a lead."

When Detective Shelley said nothing, I took this as permission to keep talking.

"Ezra and I—he runs the flower shop next to my shop—got in touch with Clive's brother."

"Staples?" Detective Shelley prompted.

"Yes, that's the one. He invited me to his house for a game of dice in exchange for information. But I think you may want to investigate him yourself. There seems to have been bad blood between the two brothers."

Detective Shelley picked up her cup and swirled it in her hands. Finding it empty, she set it back down.

"Do you want to know what I would do if I were you?" she asked after a few moments.

"I know it wasn't the smartest choice to go to his house, but I couldn't think of any other option. It was the only way he'd talk."

"I can think of at least one other," she said. "Stop interfering in a murder investigation you are in no way qualified to run before you or someone else gets hurt."

"I'm not run—"

"Someone order the yogurt parfait here?"

I raised my hand halfway as the barista set said parfait in front of my seat. The whole time, Detective Shelley refused to break eye contact with me.

"I'm not running the investigation," I said, this time in a calmer voice. "But wouldn't more eyes and ears be helpful for you? I know you're the best person for the job, but you are just one person."

"That may be true, but I am a person with years of training and previous experience. You told me yourself that teaching *Crime and Punishment* made you squeamish, didn't you?"

"Well, yes, but that's because of all the—" I mimed swinging an axe back and forth, grimacing. "Uh, gruesome details."

"I don't know how to explain to you that a real murder is nothing but the gruesome details." Detective Shelley leaned forward. "You may have gone to Clive's funeral, but I saw him at the morgue. And heck, you saw him . . . I don't want to bring back bad memories for you, Ben, but you witnessed the man bleed out. This isn't some puzzle for you to solve. A man has died, and I can assure you that my team will do our best to find the person responsible. But your involvement will at best hinder our ability to do so and at worst result in more people hurt or dead. Maybe even you."

"How did you know I attended his funeral?"

"Because I was there, too, and you certainly didn't make an attempt to lay low."

I blushed. "I just felt sick, that's all. I promise I can be of help to you. I want to show you that I'm on your side."

"Do you know how many murder cases result in a culprit found?"

I tilted my head to the side. Statistics had never been my strong suit. "Ninety-five? Ninety-six?"

"Less than half. Most stay cold."

Suddenly, I felt ill. I pushed the yogurt parfait aside.

"Very few things are on my side. From what you've told me, you have very little personal connection to the victim, nor do you have friends or family who do. The most useful thing you can do, and I need you to trust me on this, is step aside and stop putting yourself in harm's way."

Still reeling at the odds stacked against an arrest for Clive's killer, I said, "Understood. Thank you. I'm sorry to have wasted your time."

I picked up my parfait, threw it in the trash on the way

out, and began the half-mile trek back to Of Dice and Decks. Much to think about, and none of it positive.

It was almost shaping up to be a normal day at work—the first one I'd had in quite some time. Five customers came in to browse the shelves, and of those, one of them even bought something. When you run the numbers, I'd admit it's not great, but sometimes you've got to celebrate those little victories, y'know?

I didn't have time to take my lunch break. While our board game sales were . . . sparse, our coffee shop was really taking off. If you asked me, it had to do with Sophie sometimes drawing little hearts or trees into the foam. People liked cafés that did that. Made them feel special.

It was all well and good when it came to sales. But it meant that Sophie couldn't cover me so I could sulk at a restaurant, and I had to sneak bites of a warm cheese stick under the cashier's counter.

I was just going in for a quick bite when I heard Dad's voice. "Put the cheese stick down, son."

I jolted, dropping my cheese stick and stepping on it as I stood back up. "Oh, come on! That was gouda. They're like four dollars a pack."

Dad was folding his arms, and he had a bunch of papers with him. They were strewn between his hands in a haphazard fashion. The only pattern I could tell is that most of them featured gray-haired, bespectacled people smiling at the camera.

Oh, no. I knew what that meant. More business loan applications, which meant more bank appointments, which meant more hanging out my poor credit score like so much dirty laundry in front of my father.

"Are you busy?" he said.

I gestured to the shop that I was running, the very passion project he started, and which I knew was very important to him, and which he very well knew was almost never busy. "Thriving, thriving. Just trying to keep this whole thing afloat."

He peeked over at Sophie and the crowd of twentysomethings with enough pocket money for caffeine crowded around her. "Sophie seems to be."

"She's been drawing smiles in the foam."

"Good call," he said. "People like that. Right, so you clearly have some time. Wonderful. Meet me in the employee room. I've got some stuff to go over with you."

I groaned. Nothing good ever came of meeting in the employee room. I followed Dad to the employee room and resisted grumbling only when the thought of resting my feet consoled me. At this point, I would be only too glad to use the break room—haphazard as it was—just to get a little more time off my feet.

I'd forgotten about the blisters you get from a job where you're on your feet all day. I lived a very cushy life as a professor. No blisters, no daily reminders of how noodly your arms were because your barista can lift more boxes than you. You didn't realize how good you had it until it was gone, I supposed.

I gestured to the chair that was easiest to get to and then at Dad. "After you."

He groaned as he sat down, his knees creaking. "You don't realize how noisy your body gets when you grow old, Ben. It's like I'm made of Rice Krispies."

"Sometimes my back squeaks in the morning," I said. "I try to ignore it."

"Squeaks," repeated Dad, slouching in his chair. He considered this. "You should probably see a doctor about that."

"I know, but with this insurance? I'm better off letting it have its way with my joints." I leaned over, peering at the brochures in his hand. "So, to business?"

"To business," agreed Dad.

He handed me a couple of leaflets, the ones with the geriatric people that had the most dazzling teeth and probably the least dismal credit scores. These people had probably never been at a point in their mid-twenties where they would splurge on the good yogurt from the health food store and "put it on their credit card" until one year later, they were looking at an overdue thousand-dollar yogurt bill and collections was knocking.

"I think you'll find these very helpful as you consider the future for the next little while," said Dad.

That startled me out of my memory-induced stupor. I read the title on the first one. *Shady Pines Assisted Living.*

I frowned. That didn't sound like a credit union. I flipped to the next one.

Twilight Villas—A 65+ Community.

Then the next one.

Beachside Mountain View Senior Living—oh, come on, beachside mountain view? What did that even mean? Were they going to jump down from the mountain onto the beach? They would sprain something.

"Dad," I said, a mix of confusion, shock, and outrage at the stupid names these all had in my voice. "These are all nursing homes."

"Yes," he said, tenting his fingers. "How would you feel about taking care of the house?"

"What in the world do you mean by that?"

Dad heaved a sigh, a very sad and even more tired one. He looked more frail, more hunched over after he had.

"Look, I think we both know where this is going."

"It's not even April, if this is your idea of a sick joke."

"Ben, please." His sternness shut me up enough for him to continue. "I think it might be a good idea if you started looking for teaching jobs. Something local, maybe a community college."

"I quit my teaching job two months ago. To help you run the shop."

"Well, the fact is that the shop isn't sustaining itself," said Dad. "And I don't think we can save it—not before and certainly not with the investigation scaring away our usual business."

"I think that maybe we're on a downturn," I said, careful with my words, "but there will be a windfall again. There's always been a windfall."

"Do you know that there hasn't been a single improvement—not one—since 2008?" He waved off my protests. "Check the books. We've got a good selection, and the community is kind, but we're no match for the Internet."

"Not with that attitude."

"Attitude has nothing to do with it. Nobody wants to pay extra for what they can get from a faceless stranger for half as much. If it worked the same with food, the restaurants would have closed down long ago."

"I sold a board game today," I interrupted.

"Just one?"

I stayed quiet.

"More than one," I hedged. "Three. Maybe even four."

"That's what I thought. You know that this isn't what I meant." Dad shook his head, bumped into a board game with his elbow, and cursed. "Gah! They're literally suffocating us. At some point you have to look at things from a realistic perspective."

Suddenly, I found a spot on the floor a lot more interesting than looking at Dad. It kept the vision from blurring. "I've never been good at that."

"I know," said Dad sadly. "You're like me. You like fiction too much."

"Okay," I said. "So let's say I find a teaching job. You don't have to—I'm not going to let you lock yourself away in some home because you think it's the right thing to do."

"No. I'm not going to make you spend until you're my age taking care of me."

"If this is a pride thing—"

"It's not." Dad bit his lip, and I could tell he was about to say something he'd been holding back for some time. "Do you remember when Grandma came to live with us?"

"Of course."

I'd been just about to leave for college. Dad's mom had been doing very well living on her own after Grandpa died. Then she had a stroke, and the family decided it just wouldn't be safe for her to live alone anymore.

"It was nice having her around, especially after you were gone—don't get me wrong, we both needed the company," he said. "But it killed me to watch her get a little worse every day, to struggle so much that when she passed, she welcomed it to escape the pain. Nobody should have to see that happen to someone they love."

"Oh, Dad," I breathed, grabbing his hand. "I'm so sorry. I didn't realize."

"I can't do that to you, Ben. Okay? I can't saddle you with that. Find yourself a nice apartment if you don't want to stay in my house. Keep spending time with that Ezra guy. But there will come a time when my condition will get too hard for you to deal with, and I don't want you to throw your life away."

I slid back in my seat, speechless. Then, I said, "I won't throw my life away. But I'm not going to abandon you, either."

"I mean some of these homes have twenty-four-hour breakfast," he said, pointing at a brochure. "Continental. Maybe it would be like a hotel. You know how much I love hotels."

"Because of the free soaps," I said.

"Because of the free soaps," he agreed. "At least tell me you'll look it over. I've really been thinking about it. I've been praying to the big man upstairs"—here, he gestured to the ceiling, as if said Big Man Upstairs was literally hanging out in the attic instead of, I don't know, heaven—"and I think this is the right thing to do."

"Well," I said, standing up, "can you tell Him to answer my prayers for once? It's been a few decades."

Dad didn't laugh at that one. But I pocketed the brochures and helped him back up to his feet.

"I'll take a look, I promise. If that's what you really want."

"It's what has to be done," said Dad. "And therefore, it's what I want."

That might have been a somber moment, the kind that I'd look back on years from now and cry about. But then, I tripped into a shelf of board games and several—including a Connect Four, which is a surprisingly heavy game—smacked me in the head.

"The room is cursed, I swear!"

I grumbled—not walked, grumbled—Dad back into the car and came back inside, staring listlessly at the cash register and rubbing my new goose egg.

That was settled. I definitely had to figure out who killed Clive. And then I was gonna scrape as much as I could to save this business, not because I didn't want to get back to teaching. If I had to, I had to—and I was much better at teaching Shakespeare than helping customers, anyways.

But seeing Dad so hopeless . . . it chilled me. If he was getting to the point where he thought I could no longer care for him, things were getting dire. Even more dire than the state of the back room. It was time for me to get off my butt, clean that cheese stick off the floor, and solve that murder.

I called Ezra, who answered after a few attempts.

"Sorry," he said. "It's school dance season. Lots of people ordering boutonnieres."

I explained my troubling conversation with Dad to him. He listened, mostly, and made sympathetic noises at the right spots.

"What do *I* think you should do?" Ezra asked me.

I couldn't see him through the phone (like most sane people, I found video calls too awkward to toy with), but I could hear the incredulousness in his voice.

"You're the best person I can think of who would know what to do." I sighed. "It doesn't feel right to abandon the case. Not only because my reputation's on the line, but it scares me. I don't like that someone was murdered right in front of the game shop. I don't like that backpack of money, either. It feels like they're trying to frame my dad and I."

"That's the feeling I get, too," said Ezra, his voice low.

"And if they can't frame us, then what?" I said. "Do they kill someone else? Do they kill us? I feel like emotionally, I won't be free until Clive's killer is caught."

"They will be," said Ezra. "You can't give up hope in that."

"Detective Shelley said herself that in over half of all murders they don't even arrest anyone, and who knows with those statistics if they even arrest the right person?"

"Is that true, Ben? That's very bleak."

"I don't know. I guess she'd know better than us, right?" I shook my head. "I can't hire a private investigator. I don't have the money. So what else can I do? Even if it risks my life, maybe sitting around and waiting for the killer to strike would, too."

"Detective Shelley said you're no help because you didn't know Clive, right? And you don't know anyone who does?"

"Besides Dad," I said, "but he hardly knew Clive better than I did. We don't really sell collectibles."

"Sure, but maybe someone else in the area does. Nerd communities are small. Someone might know something."

"Salty Con starts tomorrow. Maybe we could visit that person's booth Riley suggested—Madelyn Kerr? Find out what she knows, if anything."

"That sounds reasonable. In the meantime, I'll see if I can get in touch with Professor Acevedo. As a fellow academic,

I'm hoping I'll be able to manage the conversation on my own. But we'll see. Shall we call it another lunch break?"

"I think we'll have to. And Ezra?"

"Yes, Ben?"

"I know neither of us can see the future. But things will turn out okay, right?"

Ezra took a few moments to respond, but when he did, his voice was gentle. "I believe they will."

"Good." I took a deep breath. "Then I might as well believe it, too. What else can we do, right?"

Chapter 15

❦

I'd found Professor Acevedo's contact information on the Westminster College website. Like Mr. Newton said, he was a humanities professor with a focus on comparative literature. Currently, he was serving as the dean of his department. Every time I tried to email him from my old college account to give it a glimmer of professionalism, I kept backspacing.

My departure from academia was abrupt and sometimes still hurt. Teaching had not come easy to me, but I had loved it for the small time that it had been my career. Even with the unsustainable salary. I wasn't ready to revisit it, even under the front of investigating a fellow professor.

If my former close friend had died in a suspicious manner, would I welcome an email essentially asking if we could talk about whether I was the one who killed him or knew who did?

Probably not.

But I did have a plan. I was clutching it in my hands with a death grip as I hurried with hunched shoulders through the humanities building. It wasn't a good plan per se, but it was what I could come up with after staying up until 2:30 a.m. the previous night. It would have to do.

Professor Emmett Acevedo's door was decorated with his name plaque and a singular *Far Side* comic. Every college department had at least one *Far Side* comic in the window. Professor Acevedo must be the *Far Side* guy here.

I lifted up my hand to knock, then saw the sign on the door. OFFICE HOURS: OPEN—COME IN.

I already knew that, of course. That's why I'd come here now in the first place. The knocking was a formality, and it was one I was reluctant to give up. Like a vampire, I didn't enjoy going into places unless I was expressly invited in. Except instead of bursting into flames, I mostly just got clammy.

I took a deep breath—Beans and me in the park, I reminded myself—and turned the doorknob.

"Professor Acevedo?"

The office made me feel right at home as a former humanities professor myself—meaning it was as cluttered as a person playing Tetris poorly and smelled like stale coffee. Likely, this was because of the several stale coffee cups scattered around the room.

A man with rimless glasses and a button-down decorated with cartoon rubber ducks was hunched over a pile of papers and looked up as I walked in.

"Are you here for office hours?" he said. "You don't look like one of my students. I usually remember faces."

"I'm not," I admitted, then plowed through with my premade lie when he frowned. "I'm a . . . visiting student. My counselor said you might be able to help me with some errors in my essay?"

"Is the writing lab too good for you?"

"I . . ." My mouth went dry. "I guess you're right. Ha. My bad. They're probably still open. I'll just—"

Before I could sprint out of the room and ruin any chances at learning new information from Emmett, he stopped me. "You're already here. Sit down. I could use a good paper to tear into pieces."

I sat down in the chair opposite him and handed him the essay I had printed out only moments earlier. It was the sample essay I used to show my students in my Writing 1010 course. It was a simple piece called "Undeath of the Author: Derrida and Bram Stoker's Dracula." I'd added in a few typos to give it that "poor unassuming student" zest.

Emmett read, but as he did so, his frown deepened. His hand crunched into the paper. By the end of it, his lip curled.

"You're not a student."

I would have been less shocked if someone poured a cup of water down my shirt and then stuck my finger in an electrical socket. I sputtered, "How—I mean, I'm—"

"This is too solid of an essay for a Writing 1010 student. Your MLA style is impeccable, and you are not only stating but expounding on literary theories, even playing with them in a tongue-in-cheek way. The errors you do make are too calculated. It's like you're doing acrobatics between they're, their, and there."

"Acrobatics?"

Maybe Emmett would be better at proving my innocence than I was.

"But the biggest tip-off," he continued, pointing at the cover page, "is that you say here you are a professor at the University of Washington."

Damn it. The only true typos were the ones hoisting me by my own petard.

"You're a professor, then. An English professor?"

When I nodded sadly, he shoved the essay back into my hands. "Is this some kind of weird recruiting tactic? I'm satisfied here."

"How's the insurance?" I asked, tantalized at this man's prospects of earning tenure before retirement.

"We have dental," he said. "And a yearly subscription to a meditation app. They added it this year to help with the burnout."

I whistled. For academia, that was practically a king's feast of benefits. How I missed dental.

"I'm not trying to recruit you," I said. "I'm not even a professor anymore. I was, until two months ago, but I resigned."

"I can't imagine why. You seem so professional." Professor Acevedo rubbed his temples. "Maybe I took too many migraine pills this morning. Are you just a horrible stress dream?"

"No." I held up my hand in a pathetic wave. "My name is Ben Rosencrantz, and the truth is—I think you might have information that could help me."

"Rosencrantz. Wait. Were you a Shakespeare professor?"

"No, I specifically avoided becoming one of those with the name." I blushed. "Well, I taught Survey of Shakespeare a few times. But not on purpose. It just happened that way."

I had two options for my senior thesis based on the semester offering: Shakespeare or Hemingway. I chose the less irritating of the two, one thing led to another, and then one day I woke up and everyone was all "Ha ha, Professor Rosencrantz, don't you have a Danish prince to chase around?"

"I knew you sounded familiar. Your dad runs that board game shop, doesn't he?"

"You know Of Dice and Decks?"

"I've bought more than a few special figurines. God, I feel bad I didn't notice sooner. Your dad doesn't shut up about you."

"Thank you. Genuinely, that means a lot to me." I swallowed. "But I'm not here to discuss my dad, either."

"If it's not about your shop, it must be Clive."

When I answered in the affirmative, he adopted a grim smile. "But how did you get messed up in all this? Don't tell me you're a suspect, too."

Too? The police must have questioned him. It made some sense, at least. If Emmett really was someone with a close relationship with Clive—even if that relationship was complicated—then perhaps there was more motive to unearth.

"I was at the wrong place and wrong time," I said. "Or at least, he was, and then unfortunately involved me."

"Did you buy something from him? You shouldn't have."

I shook my head. "No, but I was one of the last people he tried to sell something to."

"That's not really a motive to murder."

"It's a little more complicated than that."

"It always was with him," said Emmett. "That's why I stopped hanging around him. My credit score thanks me every day for it, too."

"You dumped him?"

"Well—not romantically. We were never . . . you know. Involved in that way. But sure. You could call it a friendship dumping."

Had Mr. Newton been lying to me or just misinformed? It made my head hurt trying to comprehend all this. This was like playing a mash-up of Clue and Monopoly, except you didn't even get a note card to keep track of what's been shared, and if you lost, you went straight to jail.

"What, are you surprised?" He ran his hand over his face. He looked very tired. "Clive was . . . interesting. Underneath everything, I think he cared about people—me and his mom, at least. I really do. But after she died, he put a mask over all the kind parts. It was just too much. Maybe it's selfish."

"No, just human." I took a deep breath. "I got divorced somewhat recently. It hurts. Sometimes I still miss him, even though I'm the one who suggested it. But I don't regret it."

"When I last saw him, I wished him all the best in his life. And I sincerely meant it. But I made it clear that it would have to be without me in it."

"Was he hurt?"

Professor Acevedo smiled, but his eyes were sad. "That's the only thing that hurt, in the end. He didn't seem to care at all. Good riddance, I guess."

He didn't seem fully convinced. Maybe there was still motive there.

"I wish I could be of more help," he said. "But I hadn't heard anything from the day I ended our friendship to last week when I was taken in for questioning."

It seemed like Clive was very cut off from the people who cared about him in the year leading up to his death.

"Do you know anyone who might have been in touch with him?" I begged. "Anyone at all?"

Professor Acevedo considered this. "Not off the top of my head, no. It's been too long since I hung around him. But perhaps I could contact you if that changes?"

"Yes, of course." I gave him my phone to add his contact information. "Thank you so much."

"No, of course. I don't envy you, Ben. Clive drove me crazy when we were closer. It must feel terrible to have his metaphorical ghost hanging around your life all the time."

"It at least keeps me preoccupied. I only wish it could have been something like knitting or learning to play the guitar."

Professor Acevedo laughed, then said, "You said you were an English professor. Remind me what your focus was, Mr. Rosencrantz?"

I blushed. Telling other people in academia my focus usually went one of two ways. One, they told me their opinion about the Hobbit movies (which had very little to do with my studies). Or they looked down at me, as if geeking out about James Joyce was inherently cooler than doing the same with fantasy authors.

Neither of that happened with Professor Acevedo, however. Instead, he studied me and said, "A Utahn through and through. I bet many of my students would be interested in such a class. Have you thought about teaching part-time?"

"I have," I said, "but you know how hard it can be to find a position when you're unable to relocate."

"Yes," he agreed thoughtfully. "Send me your CV when you have some time, please?"

I agreed to do so and wandered, bewildered, to the restaurant several blocks away where Ezra and I had agreed to debrief afterward.

Ezra and I planned to meet at a sandwich shop, everything about it small except for the line that wrapped around the interior and outside a good twenty feet.

Luckily, Ezra saved us a seat at the table outside and appeared to have ordered for me, as well. He handed me a sandwich wrapped in paper. I couldn't help my noise of delight when I saw what kind it was.

Turkey cranberry with cream cheese and stuffing—a full Thanksgiving leftover without the relatives.

"Is it all right?" he said, eyeing me as I took a bite.

"Incredible!" I said when my mouth was no longer full. "But how did you know it's my favorite?"

"I like to think I'm starting to understand your tastes." He grinned. "Anything new from Professor Acevedo?"

I filled him in on everything I'd learned from our visit, though it was little that Ezra didn't already know. I also told him about the professor's insistence that I send him my CV.

"I think he might be offering me a job. Or at least the possibility of a job."

"You could do a lot worse," Ezra said. "Is it what you want?"

I hadn't thought about it much. Often in my life, *want* was superseded by *need*. I needed to pay my student loans. I needed to support Dad however I could. I needed to get out of Seattle, if just to escape the unhappy memories.

"I don't know," I said. "I do miss my students. But I don't miss grading their essays. What I think I miss most is just how simple things were, before I moved home."

"A murder investigation is anything but," Ezra agreed. "Do you ever wonder . . ."

Ezra trailed off.

"What?" I prodded him.

"What it might have been like?" he said. "If we'd met under different circumstances?"

"You mean if I were still a professor? If Dad were still running the shop and Clive hadn't been killed?"

"In so many words, yes. Do you think you would have even come home?"

"When I got divorced, I was already looking for transfers somewhere else. If I'd found somewhere in Utah, I would have taken it. Come to think of it, I may have still moved in with Dad. The familiarity has been . . . strange. But nice."

"We might have still met, then," he said.

"Yes. Maybe I'd come in to ask how pathetic it would be to send myself a chocolate strawberry bouquet for Valentine's Day."

"The answer is not pathetic at all, because it ends in you eating dipped chocolate strawberries. But I might have felt so bad for you," he teased, "that I'd ask you out on a date."

Suddenly I could see this different life Ezra presented.

"Where would we have gone?" I said softly.

"Well," said Ezra, his hands tracing circles on the table, "I've always wanted to take a date ice skating."

"Why's that?"

"It seems romantic. You get to hold hands the whole time, especially if your date's bad at it."

I was aware of how close his hand was to my own. What would his feel like in mine? It's not like I hadn't ever held a hand before. I'd held Shane's plenty of times.

But nevertheless, I missed the comfort of it. No one tells you that when you divorce. One night, you have someone holding you while you fall asleep; the next, you're alone.

"Would there have been more after that?"

Ezra smiled. "Maybe. Maybe I'd have proposed."

"Lucky me," I said.

"No," said Ezra seriously. "I would have been the lucky one."

It hurt to think about this alternate life. Why hadn't Ezra and I been in it instead? Were we not good enough for it? Didn't we deserve to be happy, too?

"I guess we better focus on the present," I said hesitantly. "We're close. Aren't we?"

Ezra deflated slightly. He drew his hand back. "You're right. Sorry. I just like to daydream sometimes, that's all."

"Thank you again for the sandwich. And the company. You're right."

"Am I?"

"I wish we'd met under different circumstances, too."

Chapter 16

✣

"There's a note on the door."

I tilted my head to the side, keys still in hand. "Sorry?"

Before opening the store the next day, I'd woken up an hour and a half earlier than usual to go on a run before work. My hope was that it would clear my head. It did, but that early in the morning, there was only the fog of sleep to clear out. It would be at least a few hours before any useful thoughts inhabited the space. I planned to visit Salty Con with Ezra later, and I hoped I'd be able to have my wits about me.

"A note," Sophie repeated, tapping her finger above a piece of paper taped to the door. "It has your name on it."

I ripped it off the door and unfolded it, frowning. "Who's it from?"

"I didn't touch it. Are you sure you should, given . . . ?"

I froze, then cursed. "I didn't even think about that. Should I put it back and call Detective Shelley?"

Sophie shrugged. "Read it first. Maybe it's from a customer, and we're all being paranoid."

I agreed, though I felt no less paranoid myself, and squinted at the bold yet even text on the page:

> *Dear Mr. Rosencrantz,*
> *It hasn't escaped my attention that you've been*

poking your nose in matters that aren't your business.
You and your florist friend would in fact do well to
mind your own business.

I gave you the money. In return, give me your
silence.

"No signature," I muttered.

I handed it to Sophie, who read it over and grimaced. "It's not a customer, is it?"

I shook my head. "No, I don't think so."

"Do you want me to call Detective Shelley after all?"

It took me a few seconds to register what she said, but after a few moments, I nodded. "Yes. Well, maybe. Give me a moment. I'm going to visit Ezra. Maybe he can make sense of this."

Note in hand, I hurried down the sidewalk to Ezra's shop. I found him standing outside the front door, brow furrowed, poring over his own piece of paper.

Wordlessly, we exchanged papers and read. Ezra's said much of the same thing, directing him to leave me and my shop alone while he still knew little enough to not be worth harming.

When we were done reading, we exchanged a look.

"Step inside my shop?" he said.

"After you."

Once we were inside and he locked the door behind us, I ran a hand over my face.

"I don't know what kind of Phantom of the Opera-esque garbage this is, but I don't like it."

"No," said Ezra. "It wasn't exactly 'letters cut out of a magazine' bad, but I don't like it. We need to be more careful."

"I don't see how we haven't been," I said. "I learned my lesson at the funeral. We've hardly gone anywhere that would be strange for us to go in normal circumstances."

"It might have been someone who saw us before." Ezra gave me a meaningful look. "Someone like Staples, maybe?"

"That's still who I bet it is. The man is not well, Ezra."

Though I had listened to the recording of our meeting a few times since then and found little to go on.

"Only one way to find out who it is for sure."

"You mean to agree to meet them?" I sighed. "I know I promised Detective Shelley that we wouldn't put ourselves in danger. But if she would just listen to me, we wouldn't have to."

"I'll go with you," said Ezra. "If you need me to."

A phone call from Dad interrupted our conversation—something I knew because his contact information was saved to play "Darth Vader's Theme" whenever he called. I sighed, glancing between my pocket and Ezra.

"I probably should take this," I said. "In case he or Beans needs anything. You don't mind?"

Ezra shook his head. "By all means."

After I said hello, I heard Dad hesitate on the other end of the line. "Ben . . . are you busy?"

Was I? Technically yes, if being threatened by an unknown note-writer counted as "busy," but I could make time for Dad.

"Not particularly," I lied. "Is there something you need?"

"I don't know about need," he hedged. "Maybe I shouldn't have called."

I sighed. Dad was always like this when he needed help with something—too stubborn to admit it. It was one of those pride things. This was just how he got whenever he wanted me to do something for him, but didn't want to sacrifice his pride. It was the story of my childhood.

"What?" I said as he broached whatever it was he wanted for the fourth time and then walked it back out. "What is it? Whatever it is, it's fine. I'll do it."

"No," he said. "It's nothing."

He did it again. Fifth time.

"No, seriously," I said. "What's going on? Is it your prescription refill? I can pick it up on the way back."

"No," he said. "I just don't really feel like walking to physical therapy today, or taking the bus."

"Oh, really," I said. "So you're saying that you would like my help."

"The bus," he said in a stubborn kind of voice, "is getting delayed a lot lately, and I don't want blisters on my feet."

"Dad, you know I'm happy to help you. You don't have to justify anything to yourself."

"I don't need it every time," he muttered. "I like being independent."

"I know."

"It's just this one time," he said. "I'll pay you back for the gas money."

"You think I'm so cheap that I want, what, a dollar fifty? I don't know how much gas costs, come to think of it. I should probably figure that out for budgeting purposes."

"That explains our accounting books," said Dad.

"I'll let Sophie know and be over in about ten minutes," I said.

After I hung up, I explained the situation to Ezra.

Ezra nodded enthusiastically. "Of course that's okay. We can stop and get sodas on the way. And it's on our way to Salty Con, anyway."

A little more than half an hour later, we were sipping flavored sodas with Dad after stopping at basically the Mormon Utah equivalent of a drive-through bar. We parked out in front of Dad's physical therapy place, and the Dad in question was now folding his arms.

"Text me when you're done," I said. "Do you need me to pick you up?"

"What is this?" he muttered. "Elementary school?"

"You should know. You drove me there once. I'm just re-paying you for that. You don't have to make it all grumpy and melodramatic."

"I will make it what I damn well like," he said, walking out and slamming the door.

"It's like he was having a midlife crisis," I said. "It's not fair; I should be having my midlife crisis around now."

"Who says you're not?"

"That's true—right now is definitely a crisis of some sort," I said.

"I think he's just unhappy," said Ezra, "that he can't do all this stuff for himself. Well, that's just my take on it."

"Oh yeah," I said, leaning back in my seat. "He used to get mad at me when I would microwave Toaster Strudels for him. I just wanted to always make sure that he had a break-fast before we went to work. He always seemed so tired when he got back home."

"I love Toaster Strudels," said Ezra. "Sorry, I know that's not the point."

Moments after Dad left for his physical therapy appoint-ment—we were still watching him walk into the building and all—my phone started playing the *Star Trek* theme.

Ezra looked down at it, then back up at me. "You gonna answer that?"

I rummaged around in my pockets and pulled out my phone, frowning at it. "That's not my regular ringtone. That's my voicemail ringtone."

"You took the time to make separate ones?"

"I get a lot of student loan calls," I said, "and you know I'm not picking those up. Hadn't noticed a call. Do you mind if I check?"

"No, no, be my guest," said Ezra. "We've still got a little bit until we need to be at Salty Con."

Placing the phone against my ear, I heard—of all voices—Kit's. I'd never gotten a call from them before. They were nearer to Dad's age than mine. I'd gotten the sense that even though we were both queer—something that in a place like Utah automatically gave you a reason to stick together—Kit preferred to hang around people in a similar stage of life as them.

"Ben. I don't mean to scare you, but I'm worried about you. It's come to my attention you're delving into a community you don't understand. Board game collectors can be more vicious than you think. Look at what happened to Clive, after all."

"Ezra, pull over."

This seemed like something I would want my full attention on if I wanted to avoid getting murdered, which I did. I still had a lot to see, and you couldn't do much in life if someone stabs you to death. And anyways, I couldn't really help my dad with all the bills if I was too deceased to have a job.

Ezra had hardly gotten a block from the physical therapy center, but he pulled over by a park nonetheless. Not the best place to park. It really juxtaposed how dire things were with watching a happy family play Frisbee with their golden retriever. What unfortunate choices I must have made to get to this point.

"I want to talk to you. If you want to hear what I have to say, meet me at Of Dice and Decks at ten o'clock tomorrow night. I know that's past your usual hours, but that's the whole point. I don't want anyone listening in, if you get my meaning."

I relayed Kit's voicemail and even played it back for him to listen.

"Are you going to do it?"

"I think I need to," I said. "What Kit knows about board game collectors, I can't fathom. But maybe they do know something. And they're right, too. The board game collecting community is a lot wilder than I thought. A reason Dad and I have avoided it until now."

"I don't have anything going on tomorrow night. Do you want me to stay with you?"

Though Kit didn't want strangers listening in, they never said I couldn't bring someone I trusted.

"I would. If you're comfortable."

"As soon as my shop closes tomorrow, I'll come by," Ezra promised. "In the meantime . . . to Salty Con? We should have just enough time to find Madelyn's booth before your dad needs to be picked up."

Chapter 17

The moment I stepped into that convention and was greeted with the nerdiest geek shops this side of Utah Valley, I'll admit it. It was like I was taken right back to my twelve-year-old self begging my dad for money to take a bus to San Diego Comic Con.

Salty Con was in its fourth year. Of course they'd waited until I'd moved away to build a decent comic convention in Utah.

But as Ezra and I perused the booths, I could admit it: they'd done that and then some. On the list were a wall of panelists. You could name a franchise, and they had a big name attending it. *Star Wars*? Yes. Marvel? Definitely. If we just had more time, I'd have loved to stop at a few panels. Cosplay, even. But alas, it would have to wait for a year where I wasn't defending myself against a murder charge.

By the way Ezra was gawking at all the costumes—including a clown-shoed, spiky-haired guy holding a large key that Ezra claimed was from "the video game that defined his childhood"—I could tell he wished he could explore, too. Somewhat guiltily, as Ezra had given so much of his time over the past few weeks, I scanned for any clues as to where we might find Madelyn's booth.

But as the convention was crowded, I couldn't quite tell which doors in the spacious hallway led to where. Most of the time, there was a cosplayer or two blocking the signs.

"We could ask someone where the vendors' corner is," suggested Ezra.

"We might have to. I don't want to bother anyone just trying to have a day out with their friends, but the sooner we could find—"

Before I could finish, a gloved hand tapped my shoulder. "Pardon me, sir. I couldn't help but hear you were looking to find someone?"

I turned and stepped back several steps. Two people who could be anywhere from just-out-of-college to just-turned-thirty-and-are-having-a-midlife-crisis were lounging by a smoothie bar. One was wearing a thick peacoat and had filled in their cheekbones with too much bronzer, while the other—the shorter one—was wearing a cable-knit sweater and had the sourest expression I'd ever seen on someone's face outside of those videos of babies eating lemons for the first time.

It was clear that they were cosplaying Sherlock and Watson as depicted in one of the better-known modern adaptations. You know the one. The cheekbones were a clue all on their own.

"Watson's" scowl deepened. "Don't pay attention to him. He's full of it."

"Nice costumes," said Ezra, then snapped his fingers and pointed at "Sherlock's" head. "No deerstalker cap?"

"Sherlock" rolled his eyes. "Let me guess. Divorced alcoholic with a penchant for online buying?"

"Ha! None of those things are even true," said Ezra.

"Aw, dang it. I really thought I'd nailed that one."

"You're a terrible Sherlock," said "Watson," taking a long sip of his smoothie as if it were a drag of a cigarette. "That's exactly what I'm saying. Let me be Sherlock at the cons. Just—just once."

"We've been over this, Gerald. The costume wouldn't fit you."

"Because what? Because I'm too short. Is that what you were going to say, Rick? Like you did at my birthday party?"

I didn't know that many liters of sheer venom could fit into a one-syllable name.

"For the love of . . . that was ten years ago."

I waved my hand in hopefully a "don't mean any harm but, uh, we're still here" way. "Sorry to . . . interrupt? We were just hoping . . . we're what you could call armchair detectives, and we're working on a case. The big one."

They both stopped and gave us a wide-eyed look. Rick took out a pipe from his pocket and blew it. Soap bubbles came out.

"So naturally," he said in a fake-British drawl that was very, very bad, "you have come to us for a consultation."

"Well . . . no. We're just looking for directions."

Rick deflated. "Your loss."

Ezra shot me a look, one along the lines of, "Ben, these people deduced I was divorced. Look at me. I have never been married in my life. I didn't even know where to buy wine until I was thirty. Do you trust them?"

Rick studied my face, then inhaled deeply from his pipe. Which concerned me because I'd never seen a "non-toxic" sign on a container of bubble soap.

I made a face, and Gerald sighed. "It's corn syrup."

"That doesn't make me feel better."

"Yeah, well, think how I feel."

"If you could just point us to the vendors' room," I said helplessly. "We really don't need any ad—"

"Oh, for crying out loud. You want my advice?" Gerald pointed at me, then Ezra. "You two are not going to make it on your own. You're not smart enough, and you're definitely not lucky enough. If you can't even find a room, how are you going to solve a case?"

Ezra and I looked at each other, then back at Gerald.

"He should be the Sherlock," Ezra announced.

Rick took a few depressed gulps from his pipe. "I know. I'm just a mother bird, too afraid to let him hop from the nest in case his wings don't work."

I didn't want to even begin to dissect that, so I ignored it.

"I'll tell you where the damn vendors' room is," said Gerald, folding his arms. "But I won't do it for free."

He glanced at my pocket meaningfully, and for a second, I almost mentally checked the balance of my savings account.

But then my conscience kicked in, and it said, "Benjamin Rosencrantz, you have not hit the rock bottom that is bartering with a cosplay Watson."

Before I could change my mind, the crowd parted enough for me to read the sign above a large room to our right with the door propped open. "Vendors' Corner." I pulled Ezra down the hallway. "Let's go."

In that room was a cornucopia of nerdy delights that it took all of my restraint to not drool over. We stopped at a booth called "The Dragon's Hoarde."

On the table were a number of collectibles ranging from valuable to kitschy. A bored-looking woman wearing an Iron Man T-shirt was slumped over in the booth behind it. But it was the name below the booth sign that gave me pause: MADELYN KERR.

"Excuse me," I said. "You really are Madelyn?"

She looked at me from behind her cat-eye glasses, glowering. "And what if I am?"

I burst into tears.

"What's wrong with him?" I heard her say to Ezra.

"He's had a hard few days," I heard Ezra say in response. "I mean, we both have. Someone . . . close to us passed away, and we were hoping you'd be able to answer some questions for us."

"Close friend . . ." I heard Madelyn muse. "You don't mean Clive Newton, do you?"

"Yes, that's the—"

"I don't know if I'll be any help for you. He's not what I would call a close friend."

She glanced at me, and my face must have been particularly tearstained and puffy so as to be pathetic. It was then that she sighed, long and loud.

"I wish I could be," she said. "But I haven't bought anything from Clive in a long time."

"Why not?" said Ezra.

"His items weren't what I would call the highest quality. Sometimes, they weren't even real." Madelyn frowned, as if there were a sour taste in her mouth. "He'd always claim that he had no idea, but that excuse only worked for me once. Fool me twice, as they say."

"What was the last thing you bought from him?" I said, clearing my throat to get rid of the scratchiness. "If I can ask."

She was quiet for a few moments.

"In 2017," she said finally. "Factory-sealed copy of Tetris. Like, when it had just emerged from the USSR. It was supposed to net me forty thousand dollars."

Ezra whistled.

"It didn't. I could barely get the thrift store to take it off my hands. No collector would touch it when I went to get it verified, and it turned out that the sealing was faked. Clive said he swore he thought it was real."

Five years was a long time to hold a grudge without acting on it. But maybe Madelyn was waiting for the right moment.

"Besides," she said, shrugging. "Business is going well enough that it wasn't too much of a dent. I only paid a couple hundred for it."

"He tried to undersell me on a piece he said was valuable, too."

"It's sketchy, isn't it?" she said. "But I figured at that price,

I could only stand to profit. I was new to Utah at the time. It was one of the only and last times he fooled me."

"Do you happen to know any other people he's scammed?" said Ezra.

Madelyn laughed. "Try half the nerds this side of the point of the mountain and half the nerds in the rest of Utah, too. That's how he works. He preys on people who don't know any better and then, when they get wise, he moves on to someone else."

Like an art forger, but with games. Even while working at Of Dice and Decks for most of my life, I'd never heard of someone going to that level of effort.

"If I were to bet," she said, "I'd try to find some of the people that Clive's wronged recently. He's lucky I didn't press charges. But maybe if he angered someone enough, he wasn't lucky enough to escape from his scam with his life."

On returning from our visit with Madelyn Kerr (which, although lacking in more leads, at least let me know that the game Clive tried to sell me was likely a forgery), I found the shop quiet, save for Sophie manning the café and Leon playing Solitaire on the gaming tables. His brow was furrowed, and he didn't look up when the doorbell tinkled as I walked in.

"I'd join in," I said, in the shadow of a joke, "but it looks like you want to play on your own."

Leon looked up, tensed. "Sorry, Ben. I wasn't ignoring you, promise."

"It's fine. I just got back." I studied his face a little deeper, noted the circles under his eyes. "Is everything okay?"

"I don't know. I think it will be." He wiped his face with his hand. "I'm just a little burned out."

"I see."

Something within him awoke memories of how my students would be when they came to me about all of the terrible things that were happening to them outside of class. It used to make life feel so unfair, that they were coping with so much, and I'd wished that I could do more to help them.

"Is there anything I can do?" I asked, taking a seat next to him. "I'm only so-so with business tips, but I can listen."

He looked at his game of Solitaire and then shrugged. "I wasn't doing so well, anyways."

After putting away the deck of cards, we set up a game of the most relaxing one I could think of: Winston. The goal? To build the longest cartoon dachshund possible with the cards you are given.

"Not to intimidate you," I said after explaining the rules to Leon, "but my record is a seven-card-long dog."

"No pressure, huh?"

I smacked myself on the forehead. "Leon, I wasn't thinking. I didn't mean to add to your stress."

He gave me a half-smile. "It's fine, Ben. Unless you can offer me graphic design work, there's not much you can do to fix my problems."

I rubbed the back of my head. "Eventually, I'd like to . . . whatever it is the marketers say . . . 'build the shop's brand' . . . but it will have to wait until we're a little steadier on our feet, financially."

Leon set down a dog torso card next to the cartoon dog head I had set down on the table. "I keep telling myself, 'It could be worse.' But sometimes I wonder how much worse it will get before I can't take it."

"I know it's not my business, but Salt Lake County has plenty of tech companies around. If you'd like, I could help you find places to apply."

"Trust me, I've been trying. They don't care about my experience. They just want someone with a degree." He slapped another card down on the table. "My parents gave me a chunk of money when I dropped out a few years back. It was supposed to be a safety net, at least enough to get me enrolled back in classes if I changed my mind."

"I had some savings after I got divorced. It was hardly enough to live on for a few months," I said. "It's no wonder that yours ran out."

I placed a dog tail on the run of four torsos, thus finishing the dog, and placed it on my side of the table.

"Getting scammed into oblivion didn't really help," muttered Leon, "but sure. I guess it might have, by now."

"You were scammed?" I said. Suddenly, our game of Winston didn't seem so important. "When did that happen?"

"Six, seven months ago?" said Leon. "I bought a vintage copy of this game called Fox and Geese. Have you heard of it?"

I could feel a headache starting. Sure, I knew board games better than the average lay person. It was one of my greater passions. But if I didn't interact with a game regularly, either in the shop or during game nights with friends, I was much less likely to know about it. Was it the professorial vibes I gave off that made me think I knew every jot in the history of games? Did I need to lose the jackets with the elbow patches?

"I don't mean to tell you how to run your finances," I said, "but it might not be the wisest idea to start a board game collection when you're starting a business."

"I know that," said Leon in a way that made me back off on the patronization. "I bought it because just one copy sells for thirty grand. Sometimes even more than that. But this one was going for a lot less."

Suddenly, this story sounded too familiar for my liking. The cartoon dogs on the table may as well have been nonexistent.

"It was Clive, wasn't it?" I said quietly.

Leon's face went red, but after a while, he nodded.

"I know everyone says to respect the dead," said Leon, "but he sold me a knockoff and didn't even care that I bought it with the last of my savings. I couldn't get any collector to buy it, and all Clive said for himself is that he didn't know."

"I'm so sorry, Leon. That's a lot to lose."

"It was. It was everything." He clenched his hands around a Winston card, which bent. "I can't even go to my parents. They'd be so ashamed of me. I don't think I could face them."

"For what it's worth, I wouldn't be mad at you if you were my son," I said. "One thing I've learned about working with my dad all these years is that parents make just as many mistakes as their kids. And they've been doing it for longer."

Leon laughed bitterly. "Not this bad, I bet. My parents graduated from college. They're so, so boring."

"I didn't mean to overstep," I said. "It's just hard to see you hurting."

Leon frowned, setting the bent Winston card on the table. "You actually care about me?"

"I do. And I know my dad does, too. I wish there was more I could do to help you."

"You guys give me a place to work, at least," said Leon. "Heated and everything."

"Barely. Dad's a grouch about the thermostat. I know it's poor comfort, but let me know if there's anything else you need that I can offer. Even if it is just someone to talk to."

A customer who needed help choosing between different types of Catan took my attention and, by the time I returned to the gaming tables, Leon was gone.

He'd neglected to clean up the copy of Winston, but I hardly minded. I grabbed the cards and began to put them back in the box, but when I got to the card he had bent in half, it gave me pause.

Clive must have really scammed him ruthlessly to cause that kind of emotional outburst. I'd never seen Leon so angry, or really emotional at all. If Clive evoked that sort of rage in him in public, is it possible that Leon might have done worse behind closed doors?

That evening, we received an unexpected visitor to the shop: Mr. Newton, with a hand-knit turtleneck sweater wound so high up on his neck that he hardly poked through it.

I walked out from behind the register, my hand thumbing the phone in my pocket. Ezra was probably out for the day by now. But if things got violent, perhaps I could run into a room, lock the door, and call for help.

"It's an honor to see you in the shop, S—" I trailed off, still unsure how to refer to him. "Mr. Newton. How can I help you?"

"Perhaps we could talk over another game of Liar's Dice?" he said. "No stakes this time. I just wanted to talk."

I glanced around the shop. We were near enough to closing time that, besides a few browsers who were clearly trying to ignore whatever Mr. Newton was talking about, the shop was empty. I expected Kit to drop by tomorrow, and I'd prefer Mr. Newton to be away from the shop when such a conversation occurred, but his presence—while not welcome, per se—seemed fairly harmless tonight.

So long as he didn't stab me. Though that applied to most people.

We played half a round in silence, neither of us doing particularly well. Then, Mr. Newton said, "I suppose you still suspect me of having sent you the note? And thereby having killed my brother, as well?"

I glanced up nervously from my dice to Mr. Newton. "I . . . don't know how to answer that."

"Let me assuage your fears," he said, placing the cup over his dice. I followed suit. "If I had any interest in killing Clive, I would have done it when we were teenagers. It was much easier to shut him out once we moved away from home."

"But . . . if you don't mind me asking," I said, clutching

my cup tight enough that it made my fingers ache. "You must have known Clive had some valuable items in his collection. You weren't tempted?"

Mr. Newton's eyes glinted. He lifted his chin, but his expression was unreadable. "I was not."

"Okay." I still didn't want to make an enemy of Mr. Newton. Even if he wasn't a murderer, he intimidated me. "Out of curiosity, why tell me any of this?"

"I don't like people thinking poorly of me, even acquaintances." He swirled his cup around on the table, the dice rattling within. "And anyway, your shop is . . . nice."

"Nice?"

"It's been a long time since I've had someone to play games with. Clive and I weren't always enemies, you know. When we were younger, there were times . . ." He took a breath, as if about to say something, then shook his head. "Perhaps I could pay you? I hate to waste your time on the job."

"To play Liar's Dice with you? You don't need to do that. Though if a customer needs my help, I'll need to go."

"Of course."

"But you, like any customer, are welcome."

I couldn't believe the words even as I said them, but they made Mr. Newton smile—even faintly.

"You are a generous man, Ben," he said. "If I ever suspected you of my brother's murder, I don't now."

"You really thought I killed him?"

Mr. Newton leaned back in his chair. "No, you don't have the poker face for it. Am I right in thinking you're bluffing about having four dice facing at three?"

Later, I called Ezra to tell him about Mr. Newton's strange visit. Beans curled up next to my legs on the couch as we watched *Labyrinth*. Whenever I felt troubled or uncertain, I yearned for David Bowie in leggings as a familiar, comforting figure.

"He's strange," said Ezra, "but I think I believe him."

"I do, too," I said. "But I don't want to. It would be so much easier if he did it."

"It's been hard to sleep tonight," Ezra admitted. "I keep worrying someone's going to unlock my door and knife me in my sleep."

"I'm sure Detective Shelley will find something out from the notes."

My words hung in the air, maybe because we both knew how unlikely they were. What could she possibly ascertain from a typewritten anonymous note?

"Right," said Ezra in the tone often used to reassure people who were deluding themselves. "I think I'm going to take a bubble bath, take my mind off things. What are you up to?"

"Um . . ." The thought of Ezra in the bath somewhat distracting me, it took a few seconds to process his question. "Oh! Sorry, I'm watching *Labyrinth*. You know the old one? With David Bowie?"

"You're asking me if I know the movie twelve-year-old Ezra based their fashion sense off of?" he said. "Of course I know it. Come to think of it, I think Jareth was my first crush. Maybe even my queer awakening."

"The mullet really did it for you, huh?"

"He made it look good," Ezra protested.

I glanced up at the screen. He certainly did.

"I'll keep my phone off silent tonight. If anything happens, or you just need someone to talk to, call me. All right?"

"Of course. You enjoy your evening."

I missed Ezra's voice as soon as he'd hung up. I felt safest when I was investigating with him. At least that felt more purposeful than being a sitting duck at home, especially when whoever killed Clive seemed to be very aware of us now.

Chapter 18

❧

That next evening, Ezra and I were sprawled out around the gaming table after Of Dice and Decks had closed. Take-out boxes from a nearby wings shop littered the tabletop, most of them half-eaten and picked at as the night wore on.

"So we just wait?"

Our last customer had cleared the shop around an hour ago, and I turned the lock in the door as soon as it hit nine. When Kit knocked, we'd let them in, of course. But I didn't like the idea of having the shop door open after-hours, in case whoever had killed Clive decided to just waltz in.

The lights were a tad dimmed—we kept the backlights on but the front ones low so as to hide from our unknown visitor if needed. Of course, that put us at a disadvantage if he wanted to sneak up on us. But it's hard to sneak up on a potential criminal without being in a sneaky environment yourself. Sacrifices, sacrifices.

Beans was lying on her belly, gnawing on one of those dental treats that you need to feed Chihuahuas regularly to keep their tiny mouths clean. I'd taken her along to make up for staying yet another late night at the shop. Luckily, Grandpa was not there. Ezra explained that Grandpa was not much of a traveling cat—something that was no doubt good for Grandpa and anyone who would otherwise be unlucky enough to face his wrath.

"We just wait," I confirmed, kicking my feet back and getting comfy in my chair. "And in the meantime, I was thinking we could do a little mapping out of what we know so far."

"Mapping out?"

"Yeah. You know, reviewing the evidence."

"Oh!" said Ezra brightly. "Yes, I can see how that would be helpful."

"All right," I said, moving my takeout aside and cracking my knuckles. "To business."

I pulled a game of Clue from the shelves, took off the plastic wrapping, and slammed the board game down on the table.

Ezra winced. "Are you sure this will help? I mean . . . it kind of feels like using a Candyland board to find hidden treasure."

"How would you know that doesn't work? Are you a pirate?" I slapped the case of the board game in front of me. "Better men than us have used visuals to solve crimes. Sherlock Holmes . . . maybe others, too."

"He was fictional."

"And I wish this situation was fictional, so we have that in common." I opened the box and started assembling the board. "Do you want to be Mrs. Peacock? I'm usually Mrs. Peacock, but you can have her if you want."

"Not Professor Plum?"

"That would be a little too on the nose."

"I suppose it would," he conceded. "Pass me Miss Scarlet?"

Sure, there were classier ways to relay our knowledge than through mapping it out on the board of a beloved children's mystery game. But you have to use the materials you're most familiar with, and for me, that was either board games or classic literature. Something told me that while reading *Crime and Punishment* might lead to insights on justice and the duality of man, it probably wouldn't help me find whoever took out Clive.

"A fair choice." I put the red and blue pieces outside of the board, which showed a big mansion with many different rooms. "Let's say the board game shop is the billiards room."

I placed the figures within the billiards room—close together, perhaps holding hands if you squinted, but in a respectable way.

"I'm with you so far."

"Good," I said. I placed a green figurine on the board, just outside of the billiards room. "Mr. Green can be Clive. He comes in, he comes out, he wanders around the neighborhood and then . . . at an undetermined time . . . he's stabbed somewhere outside our front door."

With each action, I moved the Mr. Green figurine around and then flicked him over on his side.

Ezra tented his fingers, his eyebrows so deep in concentration that they almost looked connected.

"Put the knife figurine next to him," he instructed. "Sort of in between his arm and his stomach."

I did so. He gave me a thumbs-up.

"Thank you, Ben. Really helps me visualize."

"Anything for you. I mean . . ." I tried to think of a clarification that would make that sound less suggestive of feelings. "Within reason. Let's bring out the suspects."

I started with the purple figure. Purple seemed like a mysterious color, so it made sense for the first suspect to take that one.

"Madelyn Kerr?" I said. "Is she a suspect or an informant, do you think?"

"An informant," said Ezra. "I really don't get murderous vibes from her. Do you?"

I shook my head. "No. I think she's made her peace with

whatever transpired between her and Clive. It doesn't seem like she'd ruin the career she has to get back at someone she doesn't care about anymore."

"You're probably right. She doesn't strike me as having enough of a motive."

I set the mini figure aside and grabbed the yellow one. "Okay, next one. What about Mr. Newton?"

Ezra shook his head. "I still don't think so."

"Get Clive off his hands," I offered. "There's even a whole sibling revenge dynamic going on between the two of them. Parental jealousy . . . unfortunate name."

"How many people do you know that have killed someone over a name?" Ezra said. "And I'm just pointing out that you live in Utah, too, where bad names are as plentiful as essential oils."

"True, true." I scratched my chin, considering the Clue figurine. "But he doesn't strike me as stable. He's a wild card in this whole situation."

"I think he should go to therapy, sure, but I doubt anything more. If anything, he seemed lonely."

"That would explain why he's visiting my shop," I conceded.

"Here, here, let me try one." Ezra slammed the white figure onto the "parlor room" part of the game. "This can represent Professor Acevedo. You said they had a turbulent friendship?"

"Somewhat," I admitted. "But I'd put him more in the realm of Madelyn. I think whatever issues he had with Clive, he's worked through them."

Ezra pushed his figurine over.

"Which leaves the mystery person who bought The Landlord's Game," I pointed out. "And ultimately led to the backpack of money on my doorstep."

"Whoever it was has the motive—buy a rare board game for next to nothing—but why kill Clive over it?"

I shrugged. "Maybe they realized it was a fake during the trade-off? It would explain why they didn't just keep the bag of money."

"When instead, once Clive's body was found, they could pin the blame on you," Ezra finished. "I like it. Or maybe *like* isn't the best term. But I think it's plausible."

We sat there in silence, considering the fallen figures. Speaking of fallen figures, maybe I should have gone to medical school instead of the academia route. You think anesthesiologists have to throw together mock Clue games to clear their name? Not unless they committed terrible malpractice.

"I think that's at least our best theory yet, unfortunately. But at least we have a theory of some sort. Talking it out makes me feel less overwhelmed."

A knock like thunder reverberated through the room behind us. Four in a row, then silence.

Oh. Oh, no. Four knocks? What kind of maniac knocks four times? It's an unnatural stopping point. Why not five, any sane person would ask. Maybe we were tracking down a serial killer, after all. It reminded me too much of when Clive knocked frantically on the door.

"I'll get it," offered Ezra, standing up.

"No, no!" I pushed him back down as either Kit or some murderous stranger knocked four more times. "This is my burden. I'll open it."

I stood up and made myself start walking before I could work up the cowardice to hide behind a shelf. The streetlights were dim around this part of town and, without any restaurants for at least a block, most other stores were closed, as well.

But I could see that there was a figure by the door. Either they were wearing a hoodie or the winter evenings had rendered the lighting absolutely poor by this time of night, because I couldn't make out much in terms of defining characteristics. They seemed to be striking a confident pose. An aggressive one?

The hairs on my arm stood up. Time would tell.

As I walked toward the door, I turned back around after hearing the chair creak. Ezra had gotten up and was walking right behind me.

"We open it together," he said.

I smiled. It was a weak smile, but a weak tea was still a tea. And a weak coffee? Well, a weak coffee was garbage.

"We open it together," I agreed. "On three. One—"

Ezra flung open the door, and the figure strode in like a businessperson to their secret therapy session that nobody else at the department knew about but their boss had recommended for anger management so they wouldn't have to get HR involved. I knew the type. I'd worked in summer sales once.

"Ezra!" I gasped as the figure stumbled towards the light. "What happened to 'on three'? What? Happened? To 'on three'?"

Ezra shrugged, following after the figure—who now had their back turned to us. "Ripping off the Band-Aid."

"Yes! On a wound with gangrene!"

"Your insults mean nothing to me," said Ezra. "I wasn't an English major."

The figure, now fully in the light by the gaming table, spun around and lowered their hoodie.

It was not a mystery killer. It was also not Mr. Newton, or Professor Acevedo, or even Madelyn Kerr.

It was Kit. Just as they said.

"I promise that I'm not gonna hurt you," they said. "I hope I made that clear in my voicemail. I just want to explain."

"You did," said Ezra. "We've just had a rough week. Excuse the paranoia."

Kit narrowed their eyes. "I didn't know you were going to bring a guest to our conversation. But I'll let it slide, since you're at least passingly good at Nertz, and I respect you for it."

"Please, please just tell me you didn't murder Clive," I begged. "I can't turn you in. I like you."

"What? No, of course I—wait." Kit strode up to me and looked me in the eyes, which took a little neck craning on their part. "Wait a second."

"What?"

"You think I killed Clive," they said.

I exchanged glances with Ezra, who shook his head and ducked lower. They didn't want to be dragged into this. I couldn't blame them. I wouldn't have wanted to if it hadn't been a "kicking and screaming, not much of a choice to it" situation.

"No, not as such. But you must admit that asking to meet after-hours is a little sketchy."

"No. Well, maybe it is. But I just wanted to talk privately. I didn't murder anybody, all right?"

You know how in books, the main character always talks about letting out a breath they hadn't realized they'd been holding after a tense situation calms down? Well, I didn't do that, but I might have if I were in a book, because the relief took a load right off my shoulders.

"Can I sit down?" said Kit, eyeing the wings by Ezra. "I'm super hungry."

"You need to listen to Dr. Petras," I scolded them in my best faux-parent, despite Kit being at least a decade or two older than me, as they sat down by Ezra and began scarfing down wing after wing. "Isn't she always telling you to make sure you get your three meals?"

"You're one to talk Ben," said Ezra.

"I eat the leftover fries at the end of the day sometimes, but by then, it's kinda like eating cardboard."

I pulled up a seat in between the two, scooting slightly closer to Ezra. Of the two, even though I was sure (until now, at least) that Kit was a good and non-murderous person, I trusted Ezra more.

"I think I know a little bit about what happened to Clive," said Kit, "because I think I'm part of the community he was dipping his toes in."

"Which is?"

"The collectible scammer community," said Kit.

"Why is that a thing? Why is that so popular in Utah?"

"A lot of nerds," said Kit, "but also a lot of thrifty nerds. And a lot of rich nerds, cheap, cheap rich nerds that don't go to auctions. They buy things at a bargain. Even if it means they have to go to unsavory places to do it."

"I wouldn't call you an unsavory person," said Ezra.

"No, that's true. But I am a person who sells fake trading cards to wealthy idiots. You're not gonna turn me in, right?"

"Well, no, I suppose not," I said. "It's not like you killed someone. But I don't think that's the best career for you to be starting."

"It's not a career," they said. "It's just to pay electricity. Sometimes rent. I'll stop as soon as I figure out something else to bring money in. Running a brewery isn't cheap, you know, and I always make sure my employees are paid on time. Just . . . not always in the most ethical of ways."

Ezra ran his fingers through his hair. "Why, though?"

"Because it's so easy," said Kit. "They don't even really guess that it's fake. They're just so caught up in thinking that they can get this rare card for just a fraction of the price. One sell, and I'm set for a few months."

"That is pretty smart," I said, "but how do you live with it?"

"I don't really care about someone who has the extra spending money to buy a dumb little piece of paper for ten grand. If that's the worst thing that ever happened to them, then they live a pretty good life."

"Between you and me," I said, "I think I agree with that."

"What about Clive?" said Ezra.

"I knew that Clive was doing similar things in similar circles," said Kit, "but I don't know who he traded that game to specifically. I don't know who sold it, either. It's very hush-hush right now, ever since Clive died."

"Damn it," I muttered, then remembered I was in front of Kit. "Sorry. I try not to swear, but it slips out sometimes."

They slumped lower in their seat. "I'll be lucky if I'll be able to sell anything for the rest of the year. They're gonna be getting their microscopes out and analyzing everything. I'll be taking a terrible blow to my finances, I'll tell you that."

"There's always crowdfunding," I offered. "That's how my cousin paid for knee surgery."

"Great," said Kit, distracted. "Sure. That's not dystopian at all. Look. I'll ask some of my buddies, see if they know anything about the board game. Try not to rouse suspicion, though. I'll let you know if I hear anything. But for starters?"

"Yes?"

Kit kicked the ground, hesitating. "I heard . . . well, it's just a rumor, but he was supposed to be selling a collectible Monopoly game to Mark Levine."

"Collectible Monopoly game—that's exactly what Clive was trying to sell me. Mark Levine," I muttered to myself. "Why does that name sound so familiar?"

Ezra snapped his fingers a moment later. "The billboard guy!"

Oh, that was it. Mark Levine was the head of a skincare company called Beauty Mark, LLC, one of the biggest companies in Utah's snake oil–obsessed economy. He ran a series of tasteless billboards by the highway that, at their most harmless, insulted the reader's "visible acne scars." The more dangerous ones were the ones that began with, "Be Your Own Boss!"

"Yeah, him," Kit admitted. "Supposedly, he started Beauty Mark just to get out of his debt from his trading card habit. Now all he has to worry about is the massive tax fraud he commits."

"Thank you," I said. "You'll still be going to Nertz, I hope?"

"Of course," they said. "Nertz is my number one priority. Forging things is like, number five."

"What's number two, three, and four?" asked Ezra.

"I don't know," they said. "I'm keeping them open, trying to figure out my purpose in life and all that. It's never too late in life for a little introspection."

"I tried once, too," I said. "You can see how it worked out for me."

"Your life isn't terrible," said Kit. "It's a little quiet, sure, but you've got your dad. And you have us at the business owners' meeting, too."

"I'll value that compliment for the rest of my life," I promised, which earned me an eye roll.

As soon as they left, I went over to the store coffee station, turned on the drip machine, and just drank it straight from the pot. It was going to be one of those mornings tomorrow for which, to motivate myself, I might as well start getting caffeinated now.

I typed *Mark Levine* into my laptop's search bar and took another sip of coffee.

Chapter 19

The next day was our first business owners' group meeting after the incident.

That was the way I decided to refer to it in my mind. "The time that I found an especially irritating customer dead" just didn't have quite the same ring to it. It also brought the trauma of having witnessed that right back to the forefront of my brain, where I didn't want it to be.

While Dad would resume playing in my stead tonight (too many Nertz players made for a hectic game, and I just wasn't in the mood for chaos), I decided to watch.

By the late afternoon, I seemed to be coming down with a small cold. Or perhaps it was the stress catching up with me. Hard to say some days.

"Pull yourself together," I said to my reflection in the mirror, which stared back at me with a defiant frown. "You aren't supposed to get weird bodily symptoms until you're at least middle-aged."

To distract myself from my general sense of malaise, I checked on my attempted email to Mark Levine. Nothing yet. Reaching out to his business's "Contact Us" form put me in touch with his customer service team, but I doubted they were allowed to give the personal contact information for their CEO because some stranger asked them nicely.

I hated to bother him but, after shooting a text to make sure he wasn't in class, I called Professor Acevedo for guidance.

"You don't happen to know a man named Mark Levine, do you?" I asked. "I'm trying to get in touch with him."

If not, I vowed to ask Mr. Newton—even if my acquaintanceship with him was tenuous, perhaps he and Mark knew each other through similar businessmen circles.

"Mark Levine . . . yes, actually." Professor Acevedo snapped his fingers, his astonishment audible even over my phone and its so-so-at-best service. "I haven't heard that name in quite a while. Clive used to deal with him fairly often. I might even have his contact information in my phone. Mind if I check and message you?"

"Yes, of course!"

Moments later, to my astonishment, I had a number. Praying that his contact information hadn't changed since Professor Acevedo had put an end to his and Clive's friendship, I sent a single text—a bold one, to get his attention:

I know what you did with The Landlord's Game.

And surprisingly, within thirty seconds, I had a response.

Who is this, a cop?

Not a cop. A concerned board game enthusiast. Emmett Acevedo put us in touch. Perhaps we can talk?

The ". . . ." stayed on the screen for a long time as he—presumably Mark Levine, as I had no reason not to trust Professor Acevedo—typed. Then:

If you let me name the place and time, then you might have a deal. How would you like to swim?

That depends. Is that a threat as in, with the fishes?

No, no. I just have a previous engagement tomorrow that I can't rearrange. Not everything in life is a threat. If anything, you're threatening me. Did you ever think about that?

Fair enough.

Mountain Peak Indoor Water Park at 10 AM. Meet me by the lazy river.

I widened my eyes and put the phone in my pocket. Of all the places to meet a potential informant, a water park wasn't exactly the highest point in my expectations. Not this time of year, anyway. But as long as I myself did not have to get in the water, I would make it work.

After visiting Ezra's shop to fill him in—thankfully, he agreed to accompany me to Mark's meeting—I put my phone away and finished preparing Of Dice and Decks for the business owners' meeting. Everyone from last time joined, which surprised me. I put my hands in my pockets, a tad bashful. All the usuals were there: Leon, Dr. Petras and Yael, Kit, Quentin, Ezra. And Leon was tapping away on his computer as usual, with an intense focus.

"Sorry," he said, putting it away when I cleared my throat. "I've got a client that doesn't really know what the meaning of the word *rest* means."

"No worries," I said. "I certainly understand how that goes."

"Really?" said Leon. "Because the shop seems pretty dead lately, and—"

"Yes," I said firmly. "Really. Look, do you want to play Nertz or not? I know it might be kind of uncomfortable after, um . . ."

"You mean after the whole murder scene?" Yael waved her hand. "I've heard true crime podcasts that are much grislier. Don't you worry."

"Maybe I should worry for you!" said Dr. Petras, which had Yael rolling her eyes.

"Yes, well, I just assumed when it happens to you in real life, more of you might . . ." I took a deep breath. "Never mind."

"After everything that happened last week, I am in the

mood to forget a little," said Quentin. "Such awful business."

"How are you doing, Ben and Martin?" said Dr. Petras, peering at me with a sad expression on her face.

It was a question that I didn't really know how to answer. It had been quite a complicated little while. And it didn't seem to be getting any less complicated as the days went on.

I started to speak, then trailed off. "I am surviving. And that's really all that I can hope for right now."

"We're both surviving," said Dad firmly. "And soon enough, we'll be thriving, too."

"Police not giving you a hard time?" said Quentin.

"No," I said, giving Ezra a look.

"We're hoping for the best for you," said Quentin gruffly. "Both of you. Just know that."

"Thank you," I said. "That's really kind of you to say."

At the end of the Nertz tournament (which Kit won easily enough, as usual), Dad asked if there were any questions before we wrapped up for the evening. Leon raised his hand. "Shop doing all right, though?"

I sighed. "Don't worry about us. It's not the best of circumstances, but it's not the worst, either. You're a good guy, Leon. But I don't really want to discuss this with you."

"Fair, fair," he said, slamming his laptop, heading out the door. "Just let me know if there's anything I can do. Maybe drum up a few extra clients and donate the proceeds to you."

"Please don't do that," I said. "I already feel too guilty."

Ezra helped me close down the shop. Then once everyone was gone, he said in a lower voice, "How do you really feel?"

I groaned. "To be honest with you, I feel like garbage. But I'm still going. I haven't collapsed of exhaustion yet."

He patted my shoulder. "You'll keep going. You are made of stronger stuff than to stop. Anyways, we're making headway, I think."

"You really think so?"

"That's what I'm telling myself," he said. "To trivia night?"

I nodded. "I'm crossing my fingers that I don't make a fool of myself, and for once, I have a good feeling. Let's go."

Despite my outings to the Devil's Brewery's slam poetry nights as a college student, I had never been to bar trivia before.

"What do we do if neither of us knows the answer?" I asked.

"Is this your first time?" Ezra grinned when I answered in the affirmative. "A bar trivia virgin!"

"It's been a while since I was a virgin in something." After a few seconds, I realized how what I said sounded, and blushed. "I mean . . ."

Ezra snickered, seemingly unaware of my embarrassment (or at least the extent of it), and just said, "You'll be just fine. What do you tell your students if they don't know the answer to a question?"

"Well, they were often English majors, so the answer was 'BS your way into making me think you do.' Quote Derrida or something. Death of the author can justify a lot of inane theses if you know how to use it correctly."

"There you go, Professor Rosencrantz. You solved your own concern."

"Right," I said, trying to push down my nerves as we walked in.

The Devil's Brewery poked fun at the Mormon-majority culture of Utah, which forbade drinking, in a way that now overstepped into cruelty. Its mascot was a cartoonish devil with a pitchfork that felt more on the side of cutesy than threatening. Its most popular drink was a hard root beer that, while I had yet to acquire a taste for it, had its own cult following.

Ezra and I grabbed two chairs near the back. When the waiter took our order, he asked, "Are the Moscow Mules served in one of those fancy golden cups?"

"Of course."

"Then I'll have one," he said.

"I'll take . . . a beer." When the waiter cocked his head to the side, I added, "Maybe a fruit-flavored one?"

He suggested the Popping Apricot IPA and, as it fulfilled my requirements given how little I knew about beer, I accepted it.

Making the rounds across the brewery, Kit stopped by our table.

"Well, this is a surprise, Ben. I haven't seen you here since the Valentine's Day Slam of '15!"

I sunk deeper in my chair. "Can you blame me, Kit?"

Ezra's eyes widened like he'd been given a Christmas present. "What happened then?"

"He—"

I cut them off, giving myself the dignity of at least telling the story myself. "I made a diary entry about my ex-boyfriend into a collage poem and read it."

Ezra raised his eyebrows. "Well, was it good?"

"It was . . ." Kit searched for the words.

"No, it wasn't," I said. "I haven't brought any poems about Shane tonight. Just for the record."

"That's a shame. Trivia night could use a little spice." As the waiter came out with our drinks and a plate of truffle fries I'd ordered for us both, Kit nudged me. "I think you'll be glad you gave tonight a chance, Ben."

"What? Why?"

Kit shrugged. "I said what I said. Luck may just be in your corner, my young hopeless romantic friend. Things going okay with the case?"

Even though nobody seemed to be listening to us, I assumed Kit wouldn't want us to delve into the details of a murder investigation while their customers were eating.

"I hope so."

"Then I wish you luck on both endeavors." Kit sauntered off. "And if you need me, well, you have my number."

Ezra and I watched them chit-chat with another table.

"At what stage in our friendship can I expect bad poetry to be written about me?" he asked.

I stared at him, horrified.

He held up his hands. "Kidding."

I took a sip of my beer. It was indeed beer. It tasted like most beers: yeasty, but not unpleasant. Like a believer in church, I put my faith in the bartender that its intention was for it to be apricot-flavored.

Before I could answer him, a bartender who I didn't recognize made her way to the bar area with all the taps with a microphone in hand.

"Welcome to another wild bar trivia night!" she said. "Get out your D-twenties, because tonight is sci-fi/fantasy night."

Ezra and I exchanged glances. I took a deep drink from my beer and slammed it on the table as hard as I could without making a meaningful noise.

"We might just have a chance after all," I admitted.

We finished in second place, and second only because by then I'd had a few beers and thought it would be funny to just write "Tom Bombadil" as the answer to several write-in questions instead of actually racking the old brain for an answer. Ezra, in around the same state of mind as myself, thought it was hilarious.

Kit appeared relieved that at least this time, I hadn't come prepared with poetry.

We stumbled outside wobbly, but we got by clinging to each other across the shoulders. The air around us felt warm, but artificially so.

"You're blushing," said Ezra.

"Am I?" I touched my cheek, wondering how he could see it with the light as dim as it was. The night sky was covered with the sort of clouds that would almost certainly make snow before the sun rose. The only light came from the street lamps.

"If anyone should be blushing, it's me. I was useless. Your doctorate taught you well, Professor Rosencrantz."

"Oh, please."

"I bet you were good at it," said Ezra abruptly.

"What?"

"At being a professor," Ezra clarified. "You're so smart, and you get so cute when you're worked up over a book. I would have taken your class over and over, and I didn't even like college."

I considered this and then said softly, "You think I'm cute?"

He raised his eyebrows, his gaze only inches from mine. "I have eyes, don't I?"

I grabbed the collar of Ezra's flannel, hardly thinking, and pulled him into a kiss. He deepened it, his scruff brushing against my cheek in a way that made me blush. His hand pressed against the small of my back as we leaned against my car, still parked in front of Of Dice and Decks.

We couldn't stay out here in the cold. In this state of mind, we'd need a room. I'd half a mind to let him into the shop, find someplace quiet and far away from any windows, and, well . . . kiss him a little more, a little longer.

Ezra pulled back, his voice strained. "Ben. We're drunk."

I let go of him, stepping back even though it made me topple over a little. "Right. Sorry. I'm sorry."

"It's not that I don't want to," said Ezra. "But we shouldn't . . . I don't want to make you do something you'd regret."

It had been so long since I'd kissed—and longer since it had felt like that. If it ever had. But I knew he was right. And I didn't want to make him regret anything, either.

I walked him to his apartment, despite not knowing what to do once there or if I could get back to Dad's home in the state I was in. I couldn't exactly drive or jog in this condition. The best I could hope for was to stumble on home, shivering all the way, and hope I didn't make a fool of myself doing it.

When we got there, however, Ezra gasped.

"The door's open," he said.

He started to walk in, but I grabbed his wrist.

"Ben," he said. "Let me go."

"Shouldn't we call the police?"

"Grandpa's in there," he said firmly.

I stared into the half-cracked door. The lights weren't on, and I couldn't readily see a cat anywhere.

"If we go in there and someone harmed him," I said, "how would we get him to safety? Or fight off any attackers?"

"My mom and I picked him out of the shelter together," Ezra said shakily. "He's the only family my sister and I have. We have to make sure he's okay."

I searched Ezra's face. He was on the verge of tears.

"Okay," I said. "I'll—I'll go in with you. We'll do it to-gether, okay? We'll find Grandpa."

He held out his hand. I took it. It was warm and, despite the situation, comforting. He squeezed mine and, without any further words, stepped in and turned on the lights.

The room was messy in a way I hadn't seen it the last time I'd been over. The couch in particular had claw marks on it, and several herbs were knocked over.

"Oh, Ezra," I said under my breath. "This is not good."

Yet nobody jumped out from any closets and stabbed us. So unless the intruder was playing the long game, they must have left.

"I'm calling Detective Shelley," I said, already tapping in her number. "In the meantime, I'm sure he's somewhere around here."

As I waited for the detective to answer, Ezra roamed around the house, calling Grandpa's name. He opened every door. As I explained the situation to Detective Shelley—who promised to come over immediately—watching him look for his poor cat sobered me up.

"Grandpa?"

A single fluffy paw poked out from under the couch. Ezra cried out and, bending over, pulled Grandpa out from underneath.

The poor creature was trembling, eyes darting from Ezra to me, but appeared unscathed.

Within an hour, Detective Shelley and her team came to investigate—though they offered little consolation and even less of an understanding of who it could be.

"A word of advice?" said Detective Shelley, pulling me aside.

"I swear this wasn't me. You can ask Ezra if you need an alibi, but I would never do something to hurt him or his cat."

"Yes," she said darkly, though her anger didn't seem to focus on me. "I don't think you would. I'm worried about you."

"About me?"

"Don't sound so surprised."

"I'm sorry. I just . . ." I shook my head. "It was my impression that you disliked me."

"I don't. I'm just doing my job—taking the death of a human being seriously. And yes, that involved investigating every possibility, including the possibility that you were not as innocent as you claimed."

Hearing her state it outright gave me the impression that she no longer believed this to be the case. It should have been a comfort, but it was a poor one. With someone breaking into Ezra's home, whoever had killed Clive was targeting us on a much more intimate level.

If they had killed once, would they kill again? How little more would we need to do to drive them to it?

"Please know that I and my team are doing all we can. We're not stupid—and it's increasingly clear that the person targeting you and Ezra may be the same one who killed Clive. But to protect you, we need you to at least try and follow our advice."

"Right."

"And I mean that. No more amateur investigating underneath our noses. You are not Nancy Drew, and you're not nearly as experienced. If you could all lay low—try not to be alone, if you can—it would let us do our job much better."

"I didn't mean to put anyone's lives at risk," I protested, despite the overwhelming sense of guilt. "Neither of us did."

"I believe that. You were just trying to help each other. But I need you to trust me that provoking the sort of people who murder others without hesitation could lead to more, and worse."

Given the circumstances, Ezra and Grandpa slept on the couch in Dad's family room for the night—not that our home was much safer, but it made me feel better than leaving them both at his place. Especially with Detective Shelley's words.

"I hope this is comfortable enough for you," I said, handing him a small pile of blankets and pillows from our guest room. "If you get cold, let me know, and I can convince Dad to turn on the heater. He's troubled enough tonight that I think he'd let it slide."

Ezra smiled weakly. He and Grandpa—who burrowed himself quickly into his own blanket—got themselves settled. Beans stood in the hallway, ears flat, eyeing Grandpa in particular with suspicion.

I made a mental note to have a talk with her about her hospitality to guests in need. Whatever little good that would do.

"About tomorrow..." I hesitated to overwhelm Ezra with more troubling thoughts after his cat had nearly been burgled (or worse), but I relayed Detective Shelley's conversation with me to him.

"You think we shouldn't talk with Mr. Levine," he finished.

"I just don't know what we should do. But I know I don't want to put you in danger."

"I don't want to put you in danger, either," Ezra confessed. He petted Grandpa with a faraway look in his eyes. "Here are my thoughts: the killer is already aware of us, and their threats against us just keep getting worse. I think our conversation with Mr. Levine is too good to just give up. Either he knows something or . . . it's him."

"Maybe it would help to talk with him, sure. Or maybe if we don't, whoever it is will leave us alone."

"Or that. But at this point, I just don't know if giving up will stop them."

He was right. I didn't like it, but I agreed with it. I sighed, and after letting Beans outside for one more bathroom break before bed, said, "Let's go on as planned, then. Goodnight, Ezra. If you need me . . . I'm going to at least attempt some sleep."

Chapter 20

Ezra drummed his fingers on the steering wheel. He seemed in a chipper mood, despite the fact that we were about to go try and deceive one of the most powerful men in the Northern Utah area, where MLMs thrived on the power of suggestion.

Ezra was wearing a button-down shirt that, given its sleekness and the way it fit his body, seemed probably more expensive than his entire wardrobe. He had a smart brown pageboy cap and a little scarf that didn't seem like it would protect him much from the windy weather outside. Was he dressed to intimidate?

Before we backed out of the driveway, Ezra rummaged in the back seat. "I got us some breakfast. I figured we probably shouldn't go undercover on an empty stomach."

He handed me a brown paper bag, slightly chilled.

"Oh!" My stomach dropped as I unwrapped the bag, which was very much not a profession of love. "Bagels. When did you have the time to pick up those?"

"I know you said we shouldn't venture out on our own," he said, "but I woke up at four and couldn't go to sleep. So I thought, why don't I rustle us up some bagels before we head over? Maybe at that little shop near the government alcohol store."

In Utah, you have to get alcohol not at the grocery store, but at government-placed alcohol dispensaries. Everyone who wasn't a Mormon knew where they were, in case they needed some red wine for their pasta or rum for their fruity and delicious cocktails. I knew immediately which place he was talking about.

"Ryan's Bagel Hut?"

"Yes! And you know what, you'll never believe it, but I met Ryan himself. Ryan baked our bagels, Ben. I feel like that was a very auspicious sign."

"I guess so." I took a bite of my bagel and couldn't help making a sound of contentment, as it was delicious even if it disappointed me. "An everything bagel!"

"That is your favorite, isn't it? We haven't known each other for long, but if investigating a murder doesn't bring two people closer, what does?"

"I suppose that's true. It's certainly intimate." I took a bite of my bagel to distract myself from my instant embarrassment. "Maybe not the best choice of words, but you get what I mean."

"I'm not about to braid you a friendship bracelet or anything, but I'll put it out there."

"You're one of the few people I can trust," I said. "You and my dad. And if being your friend is the most important relationship that will ever happen to me, then that's enough for me."

"What do you mean by that?"

"I—forget it."

"If you say so," said Ezra, in a tone that told me he'd prefer to keep the conversation going. But he didn't press it. He drove and handed me the aux cord. "Play whatever you like."

I plugged in my phone and played ska by a band that you could just tell by their energy was wearing spandex.

Ezra wrinkled his nose. "Oh, no, Ben. You're not one of

those people who stopped listening to new music after they graduated college, are you?"

"Too good for The Aquabats, huh? Get a load of this guy—" Here, I jabbed my thumb in Ezra's direction. "He thinks he's better than ska."

"I don't even know what that is, but I'll take the aux cord back. I won't feel bad about it."

By the time we'd gotten out of Sugar House and on the highway to Provo, Ezra had taken away the cord as promised, and I had the smuggest grin on my face I'd gotten since I wrote an entire literary thesis on the *Twilight* saga. Oh, it had cost me my chance at tenure, but I still treasured how the dean had rubbed the bridge of his nose and groaned as if he had been stabbed in the sensibility.

I pocketed my phone as Ezra put in the directions in his phone to Beauty Mark's location; then I swatted it away. "Do you see that enormous building downtown?"

"What, the Mormon temple?"

"No. The largest one."

"Oh, you mean the one that is towering over literally every other building like a dystopian grotesque of modern-day capitalism?"

"Yes. That one's Beauty Mark headquarters."

Ezra took the road that would get to that part of downtown quickest and gaped. "Dare I ask how you know that?"

"How could you not? It was the first thing I noticed when I came back." I slumped in my seat. "It made me feel as if I'd done something wrong by abandoning Utah. As if I personally had caused it to fall into such terrible hands as those of questionable skincare companies."

"It could be worse." Ezra turned into the next lane, each turn getting us uncomfortably closer to the monolith. "It could be essential oils."

"Oh no, I'm pretty sure he sells those, too."

"Dang."

As we drove through downtown Provo, we found our-selves only a block away from Beauty Mark, LLC.

Beauty Mark headquarters looked, well, without a blem-ish. There were no windows, because the whole building was made out of clear glass. It smelled, even from standing out front, like cleaning supplies. Or like a swimming pool, but not in the pleasant way. If that offered any indication to how harsh their skincare products were, then I was content with the occasional breakout.

The trees outside were all the exact same size and trimmed in the exact same way down the cobblestone entry that it gave me brutal flashbacks to reading *A Wrinkle in Time* and being terrified of the demonic planet where everything and everyone had to behave the exact same. I shuddered, and Ezra squeezed my hand.

"That's not where we're meeting him, is it?" said Ezra.

I showed him the address Mark sent me. "No, no. We still have a long ways to go. But I wanted to give you a hint of what we're up against."

"You look dashing in your swim trunks," said Ezra.

While I was flattered (among other things), Ezra's compli-ment did little to distract from the rising pit of nausea in my stomach. Something about our meeting with Mr. Levine told my gut that this discussion would mean big things for our in-vestigation. Bad things, maybe. Closer to the killer than we'd ever been . . . though perhaps not as close as Ezra's cat Grandpa. But cats had nine lives, and Ezra and I only had two fragile human ones between the two of us. Most stress-inducing for me, the fact that we were in the Mountain Peak men's chang-ing room in nothing but our swim trunks.

Mountain Peak was an indoor water park in Provo, a col-lege town one county over. I rarely dared to venture here. It was the headquarters of Brigham Young University and, with that association, more conversion therapy groups than I could count had gotten their start here.

Nor did I find myself at water parks too often. The smell of chlorine stung my nose, and I felt self-conscious hanging around with just swim trunks on. It made me feel as bare and underwhelming as when I'd started teaching courses as a graduate student. Just in a different, maybe even worse way.

In terms of Utah's exports, we were top in the nation for cosmetic health and snake oil. So Mark Levine had the top two right there in his business and was likely one of the richest in the area.

I blushed and looked down at Ezra's swim trunks for something to compliment. Then I looked away in case it looked like I was checking him out. It would have been reasonable if it did, because I was.

"Thanks." I shivered. "Couldn't he have agreed to meet us at a more . . . seasonal place?"

"Here, take this." He handed me his towel. I'd been in such a hurry that I'd forgotten one, and I didn't plan on getting in the water anyways. "What's his message say again?"

I handed over my phone, and Ezra peered over it. " 'I'll be under a reserved umbrella table, two tables past the lazy river and within fifty feet of the snack bar. Do not go past the snack bar. If you go past the snack bar, you have gone too far.' What is this, a treasure map?"

"I think I see him."

Across the pool, a lone man sat scowling while looking at his phone. He was wearing a burgundy button-down shirt that cuffed at the elbows and khakis without a single wrinkle in them. In other words, totally inappropriate clothes for a swim park. His hair was similar—so sleek that I flinched every time a splash of water got near it.

When he noticed us goggling at him, he held out his index finger and beckoned us over. It was mesmerizing, less in the *awe* sense and more in the *terror* sense.

"Inviting," I muttered.

"At least we're meeting here," said Ezra. "Not like he'll murder us in broad daylight."

As we approached him, we crouched down over his table. There was only one chair, and he didn't seem willing to give it up. It must have been a hot commodity for parents stuck watching their kids.

"Gentlemen," he said. "I see you've dressed to blend in. Good, good."

"Yes, and I see you look . . ." I faltered, stunned by his semiformal wear. "I'm sorry. Why did you want us to meet here, exactly?"

"Simple. I have the kids this weekend, and this buys me two hours out of their hair."

Ezra bristled, no doubt thinking about his nieces and nephews. "You're keeping an eye on them, aren't you?"

Mr. Levine shot him a withering glare. "I am. Thanks for the parenting advice, Mary Poppins. Are we here to talk games or not?"

"One game in particular," I said. "And I think you know the one."

"Only too well, Mr. . . ."

"Rosencrantz, but you can call me Ben."

"No, thank you."

Mr. Levine pulled a rectangular item from his bag and unfolded it on the table. With the puddles underneath, The Landlord's Game was getting waterlogged.

There's no way a collector like Mr. Levine would allow that to happen unless our suspicions were correct.

"It's a fake," I said sadly.

Mr. Levine huffed. "Indeed it is. I had it appraised just last weekend. A clever copy, but only worth twenty dollars. Less than your standard Monopoly board new from the box."

"Did you know the collector?" I asked.

Mr. Levine didn't bristle like I thought he might, had he

known of Clive's recent death. But maybe he was just a good actor.

"Not at all," he said. "I found him from a Board Game Geeks listing. Usually I wouldn't play games with a possible collection piece that valuable, but . . ."

He trailed off, his eyes suddenly faraway. But hopefully not so faraway that he wasn't making sure his children were safe at the swim park.

"I don't know why I'm telling you this," he said, "but I just wanted it to be the real thing so badly. It's the piece I've built my whole career around acquiring."

Intent—check. Contact with Clive—most likely check. It still didn't square up why he'd leave cash on my doorstep, but perhaps we'd get there if I could just convince him to monologue.

If we could even get a confession out of him while we were still in public, that might just be enough evidence.

"Can I ask why it was so important?" I asked and then cursed myself. What was this, personal essay class?

He considered me in a way similar to a lion looking at a box of chewy snacks and deciding how hungry he was.

"My grandmother," he said finally. "She was the reason this whole thing started."

"Whole thing?" clarified Ezra.

"My collection, my business—everything." He waved his hand towards a window. "The Beauty Mark building taking up half of Provo's main street. Everything."

I struggled to take this in.

"Let me make sure I understand," I said faintly. "You started an MLM to buy a board game for your grandmother?"

"It's not an MLM," he snapped. "It's a way for stand-up entrepreneurs to make up to ten thousand dollars a month from home. And yes, that was the plan, but she passed away about twelve years ago. Now, it's just in her memory."

"Why did she want you to buy it?"

"It's not that she wanted me to buy it. She wasn't really interested in the collecting aspect of board games. Just the playing part, with her grandkids."

My expression softened. "I understand that. My dad and I would play Settlers of Catan most Saturday nights."

"It was kind of like that. My parents weren't really around much, so I'd bike over to Grandma's and play games. She'd always let me pick. I dreamed of having so much money that I could help her and maybe even pay my parents to spend time with me, so I'd always choose Monopoly."

"Board games bring people together," I said softly. "Make you forget the bad times for a while."

"I don't understand," said Ezra. "Why The Landlord's Game?"

"That's simple. My grandmother was our landlord."

"That seems reasonable," said Ezra finally.

"I'd read about it in a Ripley's Believe It or Not, but what I really couldn't believe was the price." He rubbed the bristles on his face, each one even and precise. "It's taken me this long in my career to find a copy at all, let alone have the money to buy it. But I suppose I didn't, after all."

"You must have been angry," I said.

Mr. Levine's face stormed over. He bunched up the towel next to him.

"I didn't know if I was angrier at myself or that punk kid for selling it to me. But yes, I was just about inconsolable when I found out."

"Wait," I said, "*kid*?"

Clive had been around my dad's age when he died. No one in their right mind would call him a kid.

"Yes," he said. "Couldn't be that far out of college. What was his name . . . Leo, maybe? Linus?" He snapped his fingers. "No, I remember what it was now. Leon!"

Chapter 21

❧

When we arrived back at Of Dice and Decks, it was quiet—
eerily so. Not a car was parked in the lot besides an unrecog-
nizable Prius plastered with geeky stickers of almost every
fandom imaginable. Sophie always took the bus, despite Salt
Lake having quite possibly the latest transit system in the
sense that it was never ever on time.

When I got closer, I could see that one of the bumper stickers was a logo for Leon's graphic design company.

"So he's here for sure, then," I said, then muttered under
my breath, "Since when did he get a Prius? Did he buy it with
his money from The Landlord's Game?"

"Cares about the environment but no qualms over killing
people. Interesting juxtaposition, there." Ezra tugged on my
jacket. "Oh, well. Bigger fish to fry, right?"

"Right," I said, with nowhere near the resolution I wish
I had.

As we ambled up to the sidewalk, I felt a chill tingle in my
spine. It was Of Dice and Decks, but the mood was off.
Something inside shouldn't be there. Something dangerous.

"Someone set the door sign to Closed," I said, pointing at
the window. "I don't think Sophie would do that. We need all
the money we can get right now, and I don't think she'd just
abandon the store."

"Maybe she didn't," said Ezra pointedly.

"Do you think Leon's on to us? If he is, what do we even do?"

"In the detective shows," said Ezra, "the P.I. usually either breaks down the door while holding a gun, or he invites the murderer to dinner and exposes him in front of all of the guests."

"Well, we don't have a gun. And I'm not in the mood for dinner." I tried to get a glimpse through the door's window, but I couldn't see anyone. "I guess we'll have to walk in and hope for the best."

"That's usually what the victims do," Ezra pointed out.

"I know that. But I'm hoping for a better outcome."

I opened the door and stepped in, breathing in the smell of new board games and chai lattes. The lighting was lower than usual, around the level that one would expect for a romantic getaway at a bed and breakfast, not a place where one shops.

Do I announce my presence? I thought. Or do I sneak in?

Ezra tripped over an ethernet cord on the ground and swore. I helped him up and apologized, while inwardly cursing myself. That solved that.

"Sorry," I said. "We've been meaning to upgrade for a while now, but . . ."

Ezra waved me off, still cursing under his breath. "Fine. Fine."

No one appeared to be in the front room, not even Sophie. Her café station was abandoned. In her thirty years working at Of Dice and Decks, she hadn't missed a day without calling Dad first to let him know.

"Okay, Leon," I said, holding up my hands. "If you're here, we're not armed. We haven't called the police."

"I even left my phone in the car," admitted Ezra.

"What? I did, too, actually—we really should have planned this better," I hissed, then continued looking around the room while walking forward. "We just want to talk. I promise. Please don't make this harder than it needs to be."

"Or weirder."

"Yes, please, for the love of all that's holy. Too many weird things have already happened to us today. I had to talk to an MLM owner about his divorce. We're good on that front."

The lights by the gaming tables flicked on, too bright and too fluorescent compared to the rest of the room. Leon was standing there. He was not wearing his usual hoodie and jeans combo that he loved so much. Instead, he was wearing a cape, a mask that covered the top half of his face, and so much spandex that it would be criminal in itself to recollect it.

"Forget this—forget that you saw me," he said, brandishing a large knife in his hand, "and nobody has to get hurt. Not even your boyfriend."

"No, please," I said weakly. "This is exactly the sort of weird thing I didn't want."

"Boyfriend?" said Ezra. "Me?"

Leon was not pointing the knife at his own neck. It would have been easier if he had been, because maybe we could have just been all, "Please don't stab yourself," and hopefully he'd have enough self-preservation to not do that.

No, he was pointing it at us.

"Where's Sophie?" I asked.

"I sent her home in an Uber," said Leon. "About ten minutes before you got here, actually. I'd tell you to call her, but the phone's here. I was able to persuade her to leave it."

Sophie always carried pepper spray with her. You had to in a city as big as Salt Lake, especially when you sometimes worked late shifts like her. Didn't she have it on her? How did she let him catch her by surprise?

"Leon," I said, trying to keep my voice level, like I hoped a hostage negotiator was supposed to do. "Let's be reasonable."

"Oh, the time has passed," he hissed. "You couldn't just look the other way, could you? Not even when I was putting in all this work to save Of Dice and Decks while you wandered around and tried to avenge the death of someone who only ever hurt the people he met."

"That's not true," said Ezra. "I think his brother Staples liked him. At some point in his life. Maybe not recently."

"How did you know that we knew it was you?" I asked.

Leon raised his eyebrows and fished his own smartphone out of his pocket. "Thirty minutes ago, I got a text from one Mark Levine, asking me to return his money and take the board game to the cops. Apparently, he had no idea it was linked to a murder."

I swore. Of course the first thing Mark would do is talk to a potential killer about a refund.

"And the outfit?" I asked.

"The mask hides my identity. And the cape hides my form. It's what I wore while I killed Clive, too."

Given that information, I thought, it really was remarkable Detective Shelley never found an eyewitness account.

"What about the cat?" said Ezra.

Leon frowned. "The what?"

"Grandpa," said Ezra firmly. "My cat. The cat you, I presume, almost killed last night."

"I wasn't looking for your cat. I was looking for you."

Ezra paled. "To kill me?"

Leon shot him a look. "What do you think?"

"Me? Never homicidal thoughts." Ezra stepped forward. "Look. It's only eleven o'clock. If you're going to kill us now, you have plenty of time to reconsider. You haven't even had lunch yet, I bet."

"No! Not one step forward, you little brownnoser," said Leon, brandishing his knife. "My vigilante justice was going as planned until you stuck your nose into everything."

"Brownnoser?" Ezra sounded hurt, or maybe he was just

pretending to distract Leon in a very misguided way. "Is that what you think this is?"

"Ezra," I whispered, nudging his foot. "Now is not the time to unpack this."

"I'm attracted to him. Not kissing up to him. I want to kiss him." Ezra pressed on, apparently ignoring how far my jaw dropped to the floor. "Are you that ignorant? Everyone except Ben knows that."

"They—I . . . what?"

"Oh, I . . . I see," said Leon awkwardly, his free hand digging into his pocket. "Well, just so you know, I'm fine with that. That's not why I'm threatening you with a knife. I'm very much an ally."

"That's good, because a homophobic murderer is the last thing we need right now."

Ezra mirrored his body language, digging his own hands into his pants pockets. Seemed like a good technique. I idly wondered if he could dial 911 from there without Leon noticing.

"Vigilante justice," I said quietly, then repeated it. "What did you mean by that, Leon?"

"You needed the money to keep the shop open. I found it for you." Leon gestured at me with his knife hand. "All you had to do was keep your mouth shut."

"That's not even true!" I cried. "You killed someone, and you ended up framing me for murder. I'm halfway out the door to jail because of you."

Leon froze, his eyebrows knit together. Then he said in an uncertain voice, "Well, I've never done any of this before. I'm just a graphic designer. I didn't mean for that to happen."

"Tell that to the detective on my tail every time I so much as sneeze in an unusual way. That's fine that you wanted to help out the shop, Leon," I said, fighting to keep calm, "but you have to understand that made it so much worse. Like, I can't even explain to you how much worse. Just so unthinkably bad."

"If you're referring to Clive, it's a miracle no one stabbed him before I did," he said. "He's cheated enough people out of their savings that if I hadn't done it, someone even more desperate would have."

"I'm truly sorry for that," I said, "but if you think I'll side with you on something like murder, it won't happen."

"All I had to do was tell him I'd buy The Landlord's Game from him for double the price, and he met me in front of your shop as if he'd just made the greatest trade of his career. What could I do? It was too easy to pass up."

Leon folded his arms, leaving us all eyeing the big knife in his hand.

"You could put the knife down," I offered. "I think that would make all of us feel better."

"It wouldn't make me feel better," said Leon.

I put my hands up and turned to Ezra. "Well, I tried. Looks like we'll just have to die now."

"No!"

Leon pointed the knife at us again from now five feet away, while Ezra and I resisted the urge to bolt right there.

"I'm not going to kill you. All I wanted to do was drum up money for you. I even sold that game to the stupidest collector I could find willing to pay the most money so you"—he emphasized that last word, poking me in the gut—"could keep your shop open. All you have to do is shut up, and you can do just that."

"Nobody asked you to kill for me," I said. "Not even a little bit. I'd rather close."

"It wasn't for you. It was for the shop. It was for your dad." The corners of Leon's eyes watered, and he looked away. "He was my only friend when I was a kid. Sometimes, he'd sit there by me after school and teach me how to draw superheroes. The shop can't close, Ben. It can't!"

"Well, I'm not using money from a murdered man to keep

it open," I said softly. "And if it comes to it, I'll turn you in and go back to teaching. Dad deserves retirement, anyways."

"Is that so?" Leon's voice gained an edge as menacing and sharp as his knife. "As long as your dad's alive, the shop can live on. And if you want to open your mouth to get rid of the money I gave you, then I guess I'll just have to silence it."

It was at this point that several different things happened: The doors swung open; Leon dropped the knife; and, startled, I tripped over a Bananagrams (ironic, but painful nevertheless).

From the ground, I watched several pairs of feet stomp through the shop—all four in police uniform. A voice I recognized—Detective Shelley's—said, "Leon Jolley, you are under arrest for the murder of Clive Newton and attempted murder of so many others that you should be ashamed of yourself. A cat? Really?"

I gazed up at Ezra, who grinned and held up his phone, dialed to 911. The call was six minutes long and counting. "I lied about keeping it in the car."

"Smart," I groaned.

"Not really. If I hadn't, Sophie almost certainly would have once she got out of the Uber and into a neighbor's home." Ezra held out his hand. "Help you up, Ben? It can't be comfortable on the floor."

Chapter 22

After Detective Shelley and her team drove Leon away, the first thing I did was sit down before the shock got to me. The second thing I did, after the last of the police unit had left the shop, was call Dad. Ezra sat right next to me, his arm protectively around my shoulder. Much better than a blanket.

As I told him all that had transpired in the past few hours, including the meeting with Mr. Levine and the standoff with Leon, he stayed silent.

"Well?" I said. "It was Leon, Dad! Leon killed Clive. What do you . . . I mean, are you in as much shock as I am? You must be."

I heard some muffled sounds on the other end, and then Dad said, "Sorry, Ben. Beans and I are out on a walk. I had to yank her back to stop her from eating a mushroom. She thought she could sneak a little snack while you had my attention."

"Eating a mushroom? Like, just growing out of the ground?"

"Yes, growing out of the ground. Do you think people are just dispersing loose mushrooms around the neighborhood?"

"Well, thank you, actually. That would have been disastrous. But what about Leon?"

"Did the police say we have to close the shop again?"

"No, I don't think so."

"And they're arresting Leon? Presumably he won't murder anyone else?"

"Presumably not," I said. "It would be hard for him to stab anyone with handcuffs on. But you aren't shaken to hear we had a killer in our midst the whole time?"

"I can't say I blame him for killing Clive. But murder . . ." Dad was quiet for a few moments. "It will be difficult to find another Nertz player."

"Yes?"

"So, I suppose we'll both just have to play from now on."

When I finished our call and hung up, Ezra asked, "How did he take it?"

"The shop can stay open, and I can take Leon's place in Nertz," I said. "So as far as he's concerned, just a normal day in Sugar House."

"Your dad fascinates me."

"I've tried for thirty years now to understand how his mind works, Ezra, and it still eludes me." Then I added, "Impossible to play Scrabble with. Most of the words he's come up with, I've never even heard—and I'm an English professor. But then I check the dictionary so I can accuse him of making things up and, what do you know? They're always there. Infuriating."

"I wish it had turned out better." He must have noticed my confusion, as he clarified, "Your thirtieth."

"Ah. All things considered . . . no, you're right, my birthday was pretty terrible. I almost forgot it happened at all, actually."

The past few weeks had almost eradicated my sense of time passing. My thirtieth birthday had seemed so significant when Dad and I had talked about it the night Ezra borrowed my car. I'd approached it with equal measures of wonder and fear—not dissimilar to my nineteen-year-old self wondering what depths of maturity and wisdom I'd unlock once I hit my twentieth.

Now, I was happy to say goodbye to my twenties. From their start marrying Shane and stumbling my way through grad school to their finish divorcing Shane and stumbling into an *actual murder case,* they had been too chaotic. Too many insomnia-ridden nights with nothing to show for them but a tearstained pillow. I longed for the comfort and sense of certainty that people said came with age.

Though if Dad were right, perhaps "stumbling through" was just a part of life. So far, all of the stumbling had led me to people like Dr. Petras and Ezra. Maybe I would be all right even if I stumbled through my whole life.

But if there could be just a touch less murder (or better, none at all), I'd appreciate it.

"It's not too late to celebrate," said Ezra. "Growing up, my sister always planned her birthday like it was a whole season. If you'd like, I'd love to try and make up for how awful it's been this month."

"Ice skating?" I suggested gently.

"Of course. You could hold my hand. I could hold the guard rail."

The shop was quiet now. Even with the police gone, it was now well into the evening. And something told me that all the commotion earlier in the day had scared people away enough that we may as well have closed up shop for the night.

"Excuse me, Ben?"

The front door tinkled, and Ezra and I stood up quickly—though neither of us had done anything worth the blush I could feel spreading across my face.

"Ezra, too. Hello to you both."

Ezra raised his hand in hello but said nothing.

Detective Shelley stood awkwardly as she slammed the door behind her.

"It's snowing out," she said. "I hope you have a jacket warmer than that one."

"I do." This was a lie. I had almost certainly left mine in the car, where it would be about as useless as it could hope to be. "Thank you for earlier. You were right about this being dangerous. I think I almost died. Didn't I?"

"You certainly stuck yourself somewhere that most professors wouldn't, yes." She cleared her throat. "Though I came here to say the same thing to you."

"You're thanking us?" said Ezra. "I thought you said we were nuisances."

"You were. And I would prefer it if from here on out, you stayed away from my cases." She sighed. "But I don't know that I would have thought to suspect Leon, myself. The case could have easily gone cold. It's not unusual for that to happen, even to a thorough examination."

"Well . . . you're welcome. Though I admit it was as much about saving Dad's and my shop as it was avenging Clive's death."

Detective Shelley snorted. "You don't think we saw you as a viable suspect, did you?"

"Well . . . yes, I did," I said, somewhat defensively, despite not knowing what I had to be defensive about. "Didn't you? Clive was found in front of our shop. The board game he tried to sell us just a few hours earlier went missing. Big bag of money literally on our doorstep."

"Of course we examined the case from every angle, and we never ruled out the possibility—but." Detective Shelley lifted a finger. "You, Ben, are about the last person I would suspect for murder. Just look at you."

"What?" I turned to Ezra, who looked me up and down and grinned. "I could commit a crime. Just ask the Salt Lake City Library."

"If anything, I thought you were framed," said Detective Shelley. "Though it turned out more complex than that. In the end, I suppose my suspicions were correct—but we may not have turned to Leon without you."

"I see," I said, watching the snowflakes fall through the front window. "We have hot cocoa mix in the kitchen. If you want, I could—"

"That's kind, but we have plenty of paperwork to do at the station. And espresso, for that matter." She nodded at us both as she opened the door and, before slipping into the night, said, "Tell Martin I wish your shop the best, and I'm sorry for all the trouble."

Chapter 23

You'd think there would be a happy ending after Leon was caught. You'd think that I wouldn't find myself sitting in my boxers and a worn-out Star Trek shirt on the computer, Googling "English teacher jobs near me."

But, well . . . life isn't always like *The Hobbit* so much as it is *The Lord of the Rings*. Sometimes, like Frodo, you have to leave the Shire, because it's not for you anymore.

This is all a long-winded way of saying that you can't magically afford everything you need to just because you caught a murderer.

We'd tabled the discussion about whether he should move to a retirement community for now. It would have been a shame, we both agreed, for him to sell his house and leave Sugar House when he finally had enough free time to enjoy it. And as I had very little savings to speak of, I needed to find a part-time job of some sort before I became a financial burden to Dad.

"Junior high teacher wanted—must have a strong stomach and sense of self-esteem," I said, then winced. "Can't tell if I'm under- or overqualified for that one."

I heard a knock at the door. I crouched forward over my keyboard, pouting. No way I was opening my door to some outdated door-to-door salesman. Not in this emotional state.

I'd had a bowl of Thin Mints doused in milk for breakfast, for goodness sakes. You can't ethically expose the world to yourself when you are in that state of mind.

The knocking was insistent, though. Sometimes the only way to get someone to go away is to talk to them and tell them to please go away. So I groaned, put on a bathrobe for that "curmudgeonly middle-aged man" effect that usually drove people away, and headed for the door.

"Whatever you are selling, I'm sure I don't have the money for—" My voice caught in my throat as my cheeks reddened. "Ezra!"

"And the rest of us!" said Quentin.

For, while Ezra was the first person I noticed in my "oh no, I'm just wearing a bathrobe" state, the entire Nertz group was there, as well. They didn't seem to mind that I looked like the physical embodiment of depression.

"You look like the physical embodiment of depression," said Dr. Petras.

Well. Never mind.

I stood up a little straighter and pulled my bathrobe tighter around me. "I do not. This is my peak self. I have never felt better in my life."

"I wouldn't go around announcing that so loudly like it's something to be proud of."

I made a face at Dr. Petras. "If you all just came here to treat me like this, possibly the worst month of my life, then . . . well . . ."

I looked around at them all, one at a time. My anger melted. All that was left was a strange hollowness in my chest.

"We'll have to close eventually," I said, half to myself. "Maybe this year, but more likely in five or so. Whenever Dad retires. I just don't have the time and money to keep it going forever."

"You could always move it somewhere else," said Kit. "You know, it's much cheaper to rent in the suburbs. The downside of that, of course, being that you'd have to live in the suburbs."

"But," said Ezra sadly, "it just wouldn't be the same without you here."

"It wouldn't be the same to Dad or me anywhere else." I kicked a rock near the door with my foot. I swore. I had underestimated how heavy that rock in particular was. "But life rarely ever is fair."

"It sure would be a shame, then," said Dr. Petras slyly, "if someone did something to help you get back on your feet. At least for a little while."

I narrowed my eyes. "If this has to do with another murder, I don't want it."

"No, this is better than another murder."

"Most things are," I said.

Quentin pulled out his phone and handed it to me. A screenshot of the fluffiest orange kitten I'd ever seen stared up at me from his lock screen.

"Thank you, but I don't see how—"

"Sorry. My girls chose it for me," he said quickly, taking the phone back. "Here, let me unlock it."

I looked at the screen again once he handed it back to me. I did a double take. I read the text on the screen again and again. And then, I wiped tears from my eyes.

"Fifty thousand?" I said in a hoarse whisper, the phone trembling in my hand. "I'd never thought people would donate more than five."

In fact, I hadn't known such a fundraiser existed at all.

It wasn't enough to keep the shop running indefinitely. We needed customers for that. But it was enough to help Dad and me get back on our feet while I settled back into Salt Lake City and found a more stable part-time teaching job.

"Are you kidding, Ben?" said Ezra. "Of course they would. Some of the more enthusiastic have even killed for your shop."

Dr. Petras put her hand to her heart. "Don't mention that Leon guy around me anymore. It gives me a sick feeling just thinking about him. And he was such a good Nertz player, too."

Ezra pulled me aside. "I have something to tell you, too. But I'd like to tell you alone, if that's all right."

"Oh! Sure." I turned to everyone else. "Is that all right? I don't want to keep you all."

"No worries. It's the community garden meeting in an hour, so I've got much to prepare for," said Dr. Petras. "We play poker for that one. And I don't go to lose."

"No problem," said Quentin; then he hesitated. "Nertz still on for everyone next week?"

"Yes, of course!"

Dr. Petras and Quentin both left with a noticeable weight off their shoulders—the unbearable pain of wanting to be standoffish, yet caring too much about your Nertz group. Ezra stepped inside, then looked sheepish.

When they had all left but Ezra, I jabbed him in the chest with my finger. "It was you who organized this, wasn't it?"

His eyes widened. "How could you have possibly known? It could have been any of us."

"It said 'organized by Ezra McCaslin' right next to the title."

A flush crept up on his cheeks as he leaned against the doorway. "Oh, yes. Well . . . I didn't know how I could help, but I wanted to. And I figured if I found enough people who could help a little bit, maybe it would be enough to keep you afloat."

I couldn't help but notice—in this, of all moments—how well his puffy coat seemed to fit him, how soft his hair looked all tousled and with flakes of snow in it from the storm outside. It made me want to . . . to hug him. To run my fingers through his hair. Not more than that, but not a jot less, either.

"I love . . ." I took a deep breath. "How good you are to me, Ezra. You treat me so much better than I deserve."

He brushed my hand with his fingertips, and despite how much my heart fluttered, I did not let go. "I love you, too, Benjamin Rosencrantz. And I hope to treat you exactly as well as you deserve."

"What was it you wanted to tell me?" I asked when we pulled apart.

He touched my cheek with his hand, cupping it gently. "I just have."

Chapter 24

❧

Later, I received a call from Professor Acevedo that ended in me paying another visit to his office.

"I hope things have settled down in the time since we last met?" he asked after I settled down in the seat across from his desk.

By now, Clive's murder—and Leon's conviction—were talking points in the local news.

"Somewhat," I said, "though business has surprisingly picked up."

"I'm not surprised. A mention in *The Salt Lake Tribune* is no small thing, even if in reference to a crime."

"It probably helps, too, that they know for sure Dad and I aren't to blame."

"Most likely. Though I bet you're tired of talking about true crime, right?" When I agreed, he said, "I'd actually like to talk with you about a new summer program for continuing learners. If you'd be free a few evenings a week, we'd love to offer you a position."

"Really?"

I'd gone to several teaching interviews, most of them for K-12, but none of them fit the hours I needed to keep helping Dad out at the shop.

"What would the hours look like?"

Professor Acevedo grinned. "That's the beauty of it. Since we're still planning the program out, you can set your own hours for your course."

"That's . . ." I swallowed. "Thank you so much. I'd be honored to join your faculty. But could you let me talk it over with my dad?"

"Of course. Just let me know your decision before the new year."

Later, after visiting Of Dice and Decks to pick up after Dad's shift, I let him know about Professor Acevedo's offer.

"But I don't want you to feel as if I'm abandoning the shop, or anything like that," I said, backtracking. "I just think it could be a good way to generate some side income."

Dad studied me, then did something he'd only done on a number of occasions—like my high school graduation, or when I asked why Mom left when I was so young.

He embraced me.

I called Professor Acevedo later that afternoon to accept the job. What would it be like returning to academia, even if after a shorter time away? I hadn't juggled multiple jobs since college. But back then, it had been a grocery store clerk and teaching assistant. Now, at least, it would be two jobs that I loved.

I was nervous, but for the first time since I'd moved to Salt Lake City, overall hopeful.

Several days later—with an ice skating date with Ezra set for the weekend—I was preparing the first local business owners' meeting since Leon had been arrested. So I spent the better part of Friday afternoon trying to choose the perfect deck of cards for the business owners' meeting. Not something I took lightly.

When I came back from the break room, Dad was sitting in the gaming table area. He was also holding, surprisingly, Beans.

Beans seemed content in his arms. You could tell, because she was doing a little half-squint, like her sheer purpose in life was to have her little head scratched like that. It was adorable. It was also confusing, though, because Dad tried to avoid holding Beans as much as possible. The most he ever did was feed her a fried egg, here or there.

He even claimed he was allergic to her, although if you asked me, he just confused "allergic to" with "does not like." I don't think I'd seen him hold anything fuzzy and cute before, but there Beans was in his arms.

"Dad," I said, almost uncertainly, "what's going on?"

He looked up, as if he'd just seen me there. I wasn't fooled. Dad was nothing if not insanely aware of his environment at all times.

"Beans seemed lonely at home. I figured I could rescue her from a dull life in your room. She was clawing at it."

"The room?"

"Yes, and then my leg once I opened the door. I didn't mind, though. Her paws aren't that sharp."

I opened my mouth and then squinted a little—like Beans, in fact—but I dropped it. It wasn't worth harping on. And anyways, Beans did seem content. She always used to get so lonely when I'd work long hours on the campus. I got the feeling she would just sit at the window and wait for me to come home.

"That for the group tonight?" said Dad, in what I assumed was his version of a nonchalant tone.

There seemed to be something more there, though. Almost like I was back in middle school and he was asking me if the other kids were nice. It made me squirm, just like it did then.

"What? Oh, the deck. Yeah! I settled on a floral-themed deck." I rubbed the back of my head. "Please don't read into it too much. It just seemed like a lucky one, that's all."

"Read into anything? Never." Dad glanced down at the deck and couldn't hide the grin creeping up on his face. "But you have to admit, Ben. It's suspicious that you'd bring up that anything needs hiding in the first place."

Well, he had me there.

"It's just a comforting design, that's all. But more to the point, why are you here?"

Dad raised an eyebrow. "Am I not allowed to be in the shop I founded whenever I please?"

"Well—no, of course you are. And I'm glad to have you in the shop—I really am—but, well . . . are you doing all right?" I blurted out.

I hadn't meant to. Dad seemed to want to do the stoic routine when it came to his condition, which I supposed was fine if that's what made him happy, but I just couldn't do it. I was, even if it was hard to admit on an outward level, worried.

"Am I all right?" he repeated, shaking his head. "You're lucky there aren't any customers in the store right now, because it's stuff like that that will run them out. People don't go to their game stores for shows of emotional vulnerability."

"Okay. Fine. But are you?"

I saw something flash behind his eyes—worry, perhaps for himself or for me. I couldn't really tell.

"I'm as fine as I've ever been," he said stiffly. "And as far as you're concerned, that should be enough."

"Okay," I said softly. "I'm sorry."

I tried to find some way to change the subject. Not just because it was awkward, but because I wanted to make Dad feel better. Maybe it was unfair of me to bring up his illness like that. After all, it was probably the last thing he wanted to think about.

"Thank you for asking," he added after a few moments of quiet. "I really am feeling better today. Someone's been helping me take my medication more regularly. Must have something to do with it."

That was the first time Dad had mentioned my routine of

fixing up his medications for him in a positive tone. I tried to ignore the tightness in my throat. "The least I can do for all you did for me, growing up."

"Sometimes I wish I had done more. But I guess I can't look back. There's no point of wishing you could go somewhere you can't get to."

He cleared his throat and, setting Beans on the ground, stood up and began hooking up her collar to her leash. "I just wanted to take her out on a walk and figured it wouldn't hurt to stop in and say hello. We'll head back now—maybe if you ask nicely, I'll even leave a pizza on the kitchen table for when you get home."

"Don't you want to stay for the meeting?"

"What happened to, 'Stay home, Dad, you don't have enough energy to be in the shop'?"

"I promise you won't have to lift any boxes. And maybe if *you* ask nicely, I'll order pizza for the group."

"I hope you're not going to try and expense that, because I won't approve it." Even though he still seemed grouchy, he smiled. "Perhaps. Though I fear my best Nertz days are behind me."

"Whatever you do, don't let Kit catch you saying something like that. They'll never let you live it down."

As Dad and I sat down on the floor, Beans gave a sneeze that resembled a tiny elephant's. Then, she curled up in a ball and went to sleep.

The second worst news I could have possibly received (the first being a conglomeration of every piece of news I'd received about Clive over the past several weeks) arrived that Saturday morning.

It was alimony from Shane. Given the circumstances, I supposed I should have welcomed every spare dollar I could get. But anytime I got a letter with my ex-husband's name on it—even if it did contain pity money, which almost made it worse—my first instinct was to burn it so at least I could blame my tears on the smoke.

Shane had only reluctantly even wanted to get married after such a thing became an option for us. All of our other friends couldn't wait to plan their weddings the day gay marriage was legal. But Shane, all he could say was, "What would change, really? Nothing, when you think about it. We're better off without the marriage costs."

As if we couldn't afford it. But you're not exactly living from check to check when you're a lawyer in Seattle. He had, however, been only too enthusiastic to sign my divorce papers. C'est la vie.

So as I took a photo with my smartphone to digitally cash in the check, I whispered to it, "I don't need you. It's nice pocket money, but I could throw you away if I wanted."

It didn't say anything, even in my imagination, as if to convey, "Of course you need it. The judge wouldn't have awarded it if you weren't struggling enough to warrant it."

I almost did throw it away, just for that imaginary argument. But then, my stomach growled before I could even rip it up. I needed the grocery money, fundraiser or otherwise. Never a bad time to build one's savings.

It's not even that Shane was a bad person. It'd be so much easier if he was.

Instead, he was the sort who wanted to make everyone happy. He agreed to go steady with me because it's what I wanted. He said yes to my proposal because he knew I wanted nothing more than to marry, to build a life together.

Of course, he never told me any of this until the final stages of couples therapy. And even then, the psychologist had to pry it out.

Ezra, munching on a bag of chips, walked in on me as I took the picture. I jolted and nearly fell off my chair.

"Gah! Who let you in?"

"Nobody has to let me in, Ben. I'm not a vampire. It was

your dad, though." He took his hand out of the crinkly bag and gestured to my phone. "Am I interrupting something? More money from the mysterious someone?"

"Oh! Oh, no, it's . . ." I fumbled for the right words, then decided I didn't want to bring up Shane. "A late tax refund. They cut professors a lot of breaks."

"Oh, yeah?"

That wasn't necessarily true, but it was easier.

"Hardest part of the job to give up. Though I guess I won't have to anymore." I set down my phone and scooted my chair closer to him as he sat down in his. "Actually, I was thinking you could use a bit of it to pick out a game? One we could play together, I mean."

"Together," he repeated, then grinned at me. "You do mean a video game, yes?"

"Of course. If I wanted a board game, I'd just check my inventory."

"I don't think I'd mind that. You know something?"

"What?"

"Even if it weren't for the whole murder investigation bringing us together, I'd still want to spend this time just hanging around you."

When I looked into his eyes, it was like Shane had never mattered.

"I wouldn't mind that, Ezra. I think I'd even enjoy it."

Afterword: How to Play Nertz

When I was twenty years old and newly out as a transgender man, I met four friends at a local trans support group: Gabe, Jude, BJ, and Kris. On the weekends and after group meetings, we would often play a card game that Kris taught us called Nertz.

I was simultaneously fascinated and intimidated by Nertz. Any game that used multiple decks of cards, I thought, was more than my brain could handle. Like Ben, I had to retake my share of high school math classes. And I'd chosen to pursue an English major for a reason: numbers just weren't my friend, and frankly, they scared me.

But over time and many Nertz tournaments, I started to understand and even enjoy the chaos. Eventually I won a few rounds, though playing with Kris was always a question of who would win second place in the overarching game. They were such a Nertz genius that they would often reach a score in the hundreds, while the rest of us were barely above zero.

Kris passed away unexpectedly in 2022. I miss them every day. I miss their queer book recommendations, their dry humor, and their deep, abiding belief in the goodness of the people they met. Whenever I think of them, I can't help but remember playing Nertz with them—the happiest of my college years. For that reason, it brings me a lot of joy to share the game with others. It helps me honor and reflect on the friends I've been lucky to have and keep the memory of those years alive.

If you've played Solitaire, the rules for Nertz should come easily to you. It's similar, if you can imagine a multiplayer Solitaire in which everyone is shouting and losing sight of the table for even one second can cost you the game. It's the sort of game where, if you don't already have a lucky deck of cards, you'll want to find one soon. It doesn't have to be a fancy one. It just has to be yours, and it has to be distinct, and it has to be lucky most of all. You'll need all the luck you can get to play this game.

Number of Players: Theoretically as many as you'd like, but if you want a comfortably sized game, I'd suggest between 2 and 6. Up to 10 if you love the sound of yelling. What a fascinating life you must lead if that is the case. You must love sitting in front of babies on airplanes. And living next to football stadiums. Do you hang around in food courts just to enjoy the sound of people chewing, too?

Requirements: One deck of cards per player. Yes, you read that right. Each deck should be distinguishable in some way. Identical decks will not do, for reasons you will discover later on. Hence the draw to having a lucky deck you use each time. It's not *just* superstitious. It's practical, too. Remove the jokers from your deck before starting. You will not need them for Nertz. But you may feel like a joke after playing anyways. I often do, but that's because all my friends are, unfortunately, good at it.

House Rules (What House, You Ask? I Don't Know. House Connor, I Guess. Welcome In. Help Yourself to Snacks in the Kitchen. Shoes Can Stay On, Don't Worry. We're Renting, After All. In this Economy, What Do You Expect?)

1. Have each player shuffle their deck. Shuffle it well and thoroughly. If you never learned to shuffle, pass yours

to a player who can, or do your best with the shuffling skills you have. You'll want your deck nice and randomized.

2. Draw thirteen cards from the top of your deck without looking. Set these aside in their own pile. Your goal will be to get rid of this pile before anyone else can. That is how you win a round of Nertz.

3. Draw four more cards from your deck and set them in front of you face up. You will draw from the remainder of the deck as the round begins.

4. Designate a person to call the start of a new round. From the second round onward, this will be the person who won the previous one. But for the first one, who you choose is arbitrary. My Uncle Mike chooses the person who looks the most like a swashbuckling pirate to go first on game nights. Often it is my husband because of his long hair and rugged good looks. And his affinity for sea shanties, which he often blasts from our car on Saturday mornings when everyone else in the area is just trying to have a nice errand run at Target and smell the decorative candles. Theater gays, am I right?

But I digress. If you can't decide who should call the round, why not go by those rules? Uncle Mike is a smart guy, and his rules are as good as any.

5. Once everyone is focused and ready to begin, have the person calling this round shout, "Go!"

6. Now is where the fun begins, but also the danger. Are you ready? You better be, because a round of Nertz

happens fast. You and every other player will be creating Solitaire-style stacks of cards from one all the way to Ace in the middle of the table.

If you haven't played Solitaire before, what this means is simple enough. You'll be creating stacks of cards within a certain suit starting with Ace. After Ace, the cards switch to numerical order from one to ten. And after that, the stacks build to Jack, Queen, and King.

Each stack will be separated by suit. You can play cards face up in front of you or cards from your deck (more on that in the next step) to complete these Solitaire-style stacks.

Any player can add to any other player's stack. They're communal.

If you play a card face up in front of you, replace it with another card from your smaller deck of thirteen cards. The round will end when a player has gotten rid of all of the cards in their smaller deck.

7. Shuffle through your larger deck one card every time and, every third card, place it face up in front of you. If you can play it on any of the stacks, do so. If you can't, continue shuffling in this manner. Once you have gotten to the bottom of the deck, start again.

8. When a player has played all of their cards from the smaller deck of thirteen (not counting ones that are currently face up in front of them), they will shout, "Nertz!" The round is now over, and no players can add to the Solitaire-style stacks of cards.

9. Separate all of the Solitaire-style card stacks into different piles for each player's deck of cards. Count out your pile, with each card being worth one point. Every

card left in your smaller deck of thirteen counts as negative two points.

10. The player with the most points has won this round, but not necessarily the game. They will, however, start the next round.

The game ends when a player reaches one hundred points after an undetermined number of rounds. Or whenever people get bored and decide they don't want to play another round. But personally, I've never been in a Nertz game where it's gotten to that point. It is a loud, stressful, but above all fun game. One hundred points, regardless of rounds, is usually how it ends.

Acknowledgments

While writing any book involves a lot of lonely evenings swearing at one's computer because the characters won't do as they're told, it is not a solitary process. I am deeply grateful for those involved in bringing Board to Death to life, both directly and indirectly.

Thank you to my agent, Jessica Faust, for believing in Ben's story and helping me develop the story's setting into something that felt close-knit and, well, cozy.

Thank you to my editor, Elizabeth Trout, for your kindness and advice to make the mystery's plot tight and the characters believable. And thank you to publicist Larissa Ackerman, copy editor Scott Heim, Sophie Melissa and the Kensington art department team for designing the cover, and Kensington Publishing for taking the Board Game Shop Mystery series on.

Thank you to the authors who came before and inspired me growing up, particularly Douglas Adams, Terry Pratchett, Eoin Colfer, J.R.R. Tolkien, and whoever all was involved with writing the movie *Labyrinth*. Your work made my childhood very happy, and it inspired me to write a story of my own.

Thank you to the Life, the Universe, and Everything symposium for teaching me a lot about writing as a teenager. I think that conference shaped the trajectory of my life, both as a writer and a person.

Thank you to my Pitch Wars mentor, Mary Ann Marlowe, for teaching me how to plot and the '19 mentee alumni for being good friends over the past four years. Few things make me as happy as cheering you all on. Thank you as well to the 2023 Debuts group. It's been a delight to cheer each other on this year. And thanks to my agent sibling, Michelle Cruz, for the moral support and memes.

Thank you to my high school English teachers for your kindness and advice, which without exaggeration changed my life.

Thanks to Gabe, Kris, BJ, and Jude: the original and best Nertz group. Except for Gabe's *Star Wars* cards. Thanks, MT—together, we survived being queer at BYU. We can do anything if we can do that.

Thank you, Mom and Dad, for everything. When I grow up, I want to be like you both. You are my heroes.

Thank you to my four sisters for humoring Mac with the board games. Thank you to my aunts, uncles, grandparents, in-laws, and cousins (all fifty-something of you . . . or is it sixty-something now? I will be honest . . . I lost count on how many cousins I have exactly around 2010, and I'm too bad at math to catch up) for the board game nights. I couldn't ask for a better family.

Thank you to my husband, Mac, for watching through the entire *Poirot* TV series with me during the pandemic, going to board game nights, and taking car rides together to see goats. And for narrating the audiobook. And for marrying me. I love you with every tomato in our garden and would marry you again over and over every single day if I could.

And most importantly, thank you to my dog, Yoda. To quote *Star Trek*'s Data to his cat Spot, "And though you are not sentient and cannot comprehend / I nonetheless consider you a true and valued friend." I know you can't read, but I love you very much. You are the best and truest friend I've ever had, dog or otherwise.

BOARD TO DEATH

CJ Connor

ABOUT THIS GUIDE

The suggested questions are included to enhance
your group's reading of CJ Connor's *Board to Death*.

DISCUSSION QUESTIONS

1. Ben is concerned about returning to his hometown in Utah partly because he is openly gay, though he notes that Salt Lake City had become more accepting than when he was younger. When you think of your hometown, what comes to mind? If you have since moved away, would you hesitate to move back? If you still live there, what has changed and what has stayed the same over time?

2. One of Ben's favorite things about board games is that they bring people together. Why do you think that is? What memories and feelings do you associate with playing board games?

3. Ben's constant in life is his Chihuahua, Beans. It's often said that people start to resemble their pets over time, both physically and in personality. In what ways are Ben and Beans similar? How do they differ, besides the obvious that Ben is not a small dog and Beans does not run a board game shop?

4. Ben is a caregiver for his dad Martin, who has late-onset muscular dystrophy. How do you think this changes their relationship? What do you think Martin is feeling when he asks Ben to return home and help run Of Dice and Decks?

5. In exchange for information, Mr. Newton challenges Ben to a high-stakes game of Liar's Dice. If your fate hinged on winning a game, which game do you think you'd have the best chance of winning?

6. Put yourself in Detective Shelley's shoes. If you were her, would you suspect Ben of murdering Clive? Why or why not?

7. Mr. Newton regrets that he didn't reconnect with his estranged brother, Clive. What do you think he would say to Clive if he had the chance? What do you think Clive would say to him?

8. How do you think Ben's career as an adjunct professor influences his amateur sleuthing style?

9. Although Ben has feelings for Ezra, his previous marriage makes him worry that romance would only ruin their friendship and ultimately lead to sadness for them both. If *Board to Death* were written from Ezra's perspective, what hesitations or worries about their relationship do you think he would have?

10. Mark Levine reveals that he founded his entire business just to purchase board game memorabilia because he had fond memories of playing Monopoly with his grandmother. Think of a time in your life when you made a choice because it reminded you of someone you loved. Where did it lead you?

11. In many ways, Ben is a reluctant hero. He longs for a quiet, safe life for himself and those he loves. But being framed for murder disrupts his plans and forces him to step out of his comfort zone. In what ways do you think the murder investigation changes the trajectory of Ben's life? How does he change?